Murder Glazed Donuts

A BITE-SIZED BAKERY COZY MYSTERY BOOK 6

ROSIE A. POINT

Murder Glazed Donuts

A Bite-sized Bakery Cozy Mystery Book 6

Copyright © 2020 by Rosie A. Point.

www.rosiepointbooks.com

All Rights Reserved. This publication or parts thereof may not be reproduced in any form, stored, distributed, or transmitted in any form—electronic, mechanical, photocopy, recording or otherwise—except in the case of brief quotations for review purposes.

This is a work of fiction. Any resemblance to actual persons alive or deceased, places, or events is coincidental.

You're invited!

Hi there, reader!

I'd like to formally invite you to join my awesome community of readers. We love to chat about cozy mysteries, cooking, and pets.

It's super fun because I get to share chapters from yet-to-be-released books, fun recipes, pictures, and do giveaways with the people who enjoy my stories the most.

So whether you're a new reader or you've been enjoying my stories for a while, you can catch up with other like-minded readers, and get lots of cool content by visiting my website at *www.rosiepointbooks.com* and signing up for my mailing list.

Or simply search for me on *www.bookbub.com* and follow me there.

I look forward to getting to know you better.

Let's get into the story!

Yours,
Rosie

One

"ARE YOU TRYING TO CHOKE ME?" THE VOICE whip-snapped over the chattering crowd gathered in front of the food truck's open window.

I scanned the crowd, searching for the source of the disturbance, but no one stood out. Then again, it was pretty difficult to pick anyone out in the crowd. Bee and I had just arrived in Muffin, Massachusetts and set up our truck in front of the duck pond. Customers had swarmed in the minute we'd opened up 'shop,' and we hadn't stopped selling our special of the week since.

The strawberry glazed donuts were a bestseller.

"Did you hear that?" I asked my baking bestie, Bee.

"No. Hear what?" Bee had tied back her silver-gray hair today, and wore her signature Bite-sized Bakery apron, striped in pastel green and pink over a thick cream sweater.

She was halfway through a transaction, handing over a donut to a waiting customer. "Hear what, Ruby?"

"They're trying to choke me!" The voice came again. A woman speaking, for sure, but she didn't sound in distress. She was... angry.

A flash of red, followed by a few 'ows' and 'heys' caught my attention. An overweight woman in a turquoise tent of a dress, her hair dyed a shade of crimson that had come from a bottle, elbowed members of the crowd left and right. She stomped on feet, her blue eyes blazing hatred and locked onto me.

What on earth? What have I done?

"Bee," I said. "We've got a code red incoming."

"Excuse your pun," Bee replied.

Code red was our way of saying a dissatisfied customer was inbound. That or we'd just witnessed a fight, a murder, or walked in on a dead body. All occurrences that had been frequent during our time in Carmel Springs, Maine.

Oof, I have to stop thinking about that town. Ever since we'd left after Christmas, my heart had been trapped back in Maine. Which wasn't part of the plan—it was time to move on. That was the reason I'd gotten a food truck in the first place.

The redheaded firecracker reached the counter. She slapped a donut down onto it, smooshing crumbs and glaze everywhere. The customer in the line next to her flinched away, staring.

"Ma'am?"

"You're trying to choke me," the woman erupted, pointing a crimson fingernail at me. "You and your disgusting donuts."

"Excuse me, could you please lower your voice? You're upsetting the other customers," I said.

"Upsetting the other..." The woman's cheeks pinked. "Upsetting them? Who cares about them? What about me?"

"What's the problem?" Bee asked, always to the point. She didn't take kindly to being yelled, and she was protective of me.

"There's a fly in my donut," the woman said, pointing at the ruined treat. "Right there, see?"

I peered over at the flat counter and the crumbs spread across it. Pieces of the donut had been scattered everywhere, but there was no fly. I opened my mouth to tell her so, but that probably wouldn't go well.

And the other customers had started getting antsy. The last thing I needed was another repeat of our first weeks in the last town. We'd gotten involved in a murder, and that had changed the public's opinion of us at first.

A fly in the donut glaze wasn't as bad, but it was still a

reason not to visit the truck. I had to handle this perfectly. Diplomatically. I had to—

"There's no fly in that donut," Bee announced.

The woman glared. "How dare you. Are you calling me a liar?"

"That's exactly what I'm calling you."

The redhead gaped, her mouth opening and shutting. The other customers were just as round-eyed.

I patted the air in Bee's direction then turned back to the lady. "I'm sorry, what's your name?"

"Misty," she said. "Misty Murphy."

"It's nice to meet you, Miss Murphy. My name is Ruby and this is Bee. We're new to town. If there was a bug in your donut, I'd be happy to provide you with another one. Would that work for you? Free of charge?"

Misty gritted her teeth. "No. I don't want your disgusting donuts. You're horrible bakers. Your donuts are stale, anyway."

"That's not true," Bee growled. "We baked them fresh this morning. You're—"

"Bee." I had to keep things calm. It wasn't easy—the words had brought an angry boil in my veins. "Miss Murphy, I'd like to—"

"Save your breath." Misty shoved her hand toward me. "You've got nothing interesting to say." She stormed off, her red hair glinting in the watery sunlight.

A silence followed her departure. Then the gossiping started.

I pinched the bridge of my nose, forcing myself to take deep breaths.

"What a horrendous person," Bee said, and accepted money from the customer in front of her.

She wasn't wrong, but there was no use crying over... spilled donut?

"I'd better clean up this mess." I hurried past Bee and out of the truck. What a terrible start to our first day in Muffin. I'd hoped the friendly name of the town would carry over to the attitude of the locals.

I made quick work of dusting off the counter, apologizing to the customers lining up next to me.

One of them, a young woman with sparkling blue eyes like two gems in her pale face, greeted me with a warm smile. She was pretty enough to be a model, her golden hair in a bun atop her head. "Hello," she said, stepping out of the line and touching my arm.

"Hi. May I help you with something?"

"Oh, no, no, I'll join the line again for a cupcake, but I just wanted to talk to you about Misty."

"Misty?" I asked. "What about her?"

"Well, I wanted you to know that you shouldn't take her terrible behavior seriously," the blonde woman said. "Most of the people in Muffin don't really like her. And I know that's a terrible thing to say, but after what she said to you, I just wanted you to understand that no one takes her seriously."

"Oh," I said. "Oh, all right." I wasn't quite sure what to say. But I was definitely intrigued. *This is not another case to investigate, Holmes. Keep it together.* "Thanks for trying to set me at ease," I said. "I'm Ruby by the way." I brushed off my hand and presented it.

"Harper Kelly." She tugged on her ear, shyly. Her fingers were splotched with what looked like blue and yellow paint. "It's lovely to meet you and to have baked goods in town. We've had a serious lack of anything sweet like this lately."

"Why's that?" I asked, stepping away from the truck so that the other customers could file in and place their orders with Bee.

"Well, because of Misty," Harper said. "She owns the local bakery, but she's truly terrible at baking. No one wants to go there anymore. The Honey Bun in the center of town? Yeah, it's in the perfect spot to bring in business but... I had a donut from there the other day, and it had mold growing on it. Swore I'd never go back."

Eugh. That explained why Misty had thrown a full-blown adult tantrum about our donuts.

Harper shook her head. "People are saying Misty's dangerous—her father is the mayor—but I don't believe that for a second. She's just a sour woman who can't get her way."

"It sounds like she's gotten to you."

"Oh, she's gotten to everyone. Never has a nice thing to say." Harper tittered a laugh. "But what can we do?" She sighed. "We're stuck with her. I only hope that no one gets food poisoning from her bakery. I wouldn't want anyone to get hurt."

The information was a lot to process. I looked around, but Misty Murphy was long gone. "Can I get you something to eat?" I asked. "A cupcake, you said? No mold, I promise."

"That would be lovely," Harper said, rewarding me with another sugary smile.

Muffin already wasn't what I'd expected or hoped for. I got the feeling that things were going to be just as interesting here as they'd been in Carmel Springs. Was that a good or a bad thing?

Heavens, only time would tell.

Two

"You don't have to do this, Ruby," Bee said, tucking her hair behind her prominent ears. "I don't think the woman deserves any donuts, let alone your time."

It was late afternoon on the truck, and we were finally closing up after an eventful day. Thankfully, Misty hadn't come back to see us again, but she'd still been on my mind. I was curious about her bakery—after all, it would make sense that if she was the competition, I should probably check the place out.

I grasped a box of Bite-sized Bakery donuts to my chest, admiring the sunset over the duck pond. Muffin was as quaint as it had looked when we'd researched it online—a small town with brick sidewalks, removed from the ocean, but with a little pond and park, and a forest on its outskirts. This was the type of town that had boutique shops and cutesy restaurants, and I couldn't wait to explore it.

"You know," Bee said, "we still have to check in at the inn."

"I'll catch up with you there." I brought my phone out of the pocket of my apron. "All I need is the name."

"The Runaway Inn," Bee said.

"Noted. And I'm going to the Honey Bun Bakery if you need to catch up with me for whatever reason."

"I still don't see why."

"We need to start out our sales stint in this town with a feeling of good will," I replied. "And if that means bringing Misty some donuts and buttering her up, then so be it."

"I think you mean glazing her up. And I still don't agree with this. I don't like the woman. She tried to chase off our customers." Bee was positively mutinous. Mess with the truck or her friends, and she'd go to the ends of the earth to ensure the perpetrator paid for what they'd done.

"I'm going, Bee," I said, laughing.

"Fine. Fine. Just try not to find any dead bodies this time."

"Yuck. Don't jinx me." I set off down the sidewalk adjacent to the truck and took a left, winding my way past wrought-iron lampposts and brick buildings. I passed a candy store with pin-striped overhangs and window planters waiting for the first flowers of spring.

The people I passed by smiled or nodded, others, mostly teenagers, were wrapped up in conversations or scrolling on their phones. It was such a pleasant afternoon, I was tempted to take a seat on one of the benches next to a lamppost and have a donut myself.

But that wouldn't help the 'argument with the baker' situation—the only baker in town, if Harper Kelly was to be believed. There was another reason I didn't want to get on this Misty's bad side—we likely wouldn't hang around for long in this town, but for the time we were here, if there was a way I could help her business and mine at the same time, why not?

Especially if what Harper had said was true. If Misty's bakery was in trouble, there might've been a way I could contribute. If I told Bee that, she'd think I was a bleeding heart.

I frowned, turned in a circle and sought out the Honey Bun Bakery, but it certainly wasn't in the central street that ran through the town—Gallop Road.

"Excuse me," I said, tapping a lady on the arm. "Do you know where I can find the Honey Bun Bakery?"

The elderly woman pulled a face. "Sure. It's right around the corner that way. But, dear, I wouldn't go in there if I were you. I heard Malory Jones got sick after eating one of their cream cookies."

"Thank you." I offered her a smile then started off for the bakery.

Apparently, Misty had more trouble than Harper had let on. It was no wonder she'd come to the truck this morning and freaked out. She was probably under a lot of pressure—that didn't make the behavior right, of course, but I could understand the stress.

My food truck had been trashed last year.

I entered the side street off Gallop and stalled after a few steps.

It was strangely dingy here—with the Honey Bun the main feature on the curving street. The windows of the store next to it were empty, and the buildings opposite were clothing stores that had seen better days. They were already closed, and the card signs in their windows were faded.

It was like I'd stepped out of a sunny street and into a different town. Clouds rolled in overhead, and I half-expected a rumble of thunder, a lightning crack, and the sudden appearance of a masked stranger in the shadowy alley between the bakery and the empty shop next to it.

"Well, all right then," I whispered, tapping my fingers on the box.

The bakery's glass front door was closed and one of

the letters of its sign had fallen off—it read the 'Hone Bun Bakery.' The lights were on inside, though, and the placard in the door read 'OPEN.'

There was no queue leading out of the store, and, honestly, the inside of the place looked pretty dead.

I opened the door, slowly, my eyes narrowed.

"Misty, are you in—?" The words got lost in my throat.

The box dropped from my numb fingertips and hit the floor. Donuts burst from it and rolled in every direction.

Right in front of me, in the center of the cracked linoleum bakery floor, lay Misty Murphy, facedown, a knife sticking from her back.

The scream tore out of my throat before I could stop it, and I backpedaled, slamming into the bakery door. I wrenched it open and rushed into the street, heat thumping through my head. Before Carmel Springs, and when I'd first encountered a dead body, I'd been beyond squeamish.

But over the months I'd spent in the small town, I'd grown accustomed to the sights and horrors of a murder mystery. Why was I shocked now, then?

This was the last thing I'd expected. Muffin, like any other small town, had its dark and dangerous secrets.

I slipped my phone out of my apron and dialed 911.

Three

Bee and I sat side-by-side on one of the benches in the street—I'd called her moments after reporting Misty's untimely demise to the cops. She patted me on the arm, occasionally, but switched out the consoling attitude for a snort or a shake of her head once in a while.

"What did I say about discovering a dead body?" Bee whispered, as another policeman rushed by, heading toward the crime scene that had been cordoned off behind us.

"Hey," I replied, "this was hardly intentional."

"Still, you just *had* to go take the mean woman donuts," Bee sighed. "Bless your heart and soul, Ruby, you're too good for people like this Misty woman."

"I can't believe she's dead."

"I can." Bee pursed her lips. "If she treated you like dirt, just imagine how she acts with people she knows. That kind of wanton disregard is often met with a sticky end."

I paled. "I was just getting used to the peace and quiet of not having witnessed a murder."

"Here we go again," Bee said, in that resigned tone. "Another mystery that's fallen into our laps. It's like we're magnets for mayhem."

I didn't answer her, though it certainly seemed that way.

"You know what this looks like, don't you?" Bee asked.

"Don't tell me. I seem suspicious again?"

"Let's think about it for a second." She had lowered her voice as officers swarmed past us—one of them had told us to wait until a detective could be spared to take our statements and had promptly retreated to his cruiser where he sat, staring. As if he thought we'd run.

"Don't say it, Bee."

But my best friend in baking wouldn't be discouraged. "You had an argument with Misty, people witnessed it, and now, you're at the scene of the crime with a box of donuts that you managed to drop in there next to her corpse."

I slapped a hand to my mouth to keep from gagging.

"Since when are you squeamish again?" Bee asked.

"You argued with her too," I said, from behind my hand. "And how could anyone think that a minor disagreement would be a motive for murder?"

"Hmm." Bee tapped her chin. "Rubes, you know that there's just about every type of motivation for murder and that there's an abundance of crazy people in the world. The police will be thinking that too. The newcomer baker arrives and suddenly the old baker, who was seen fighting with her might I add, has been stabbed in the back."

"I know. I know, all right? But that doesn't mean I have to like it."

"Good," Bee said. "Because you're going to have to overcome your squeamishness about this if you want us to solve the case."

"Us?" I gaped at her. "Not again, Bee."

"You trust that these cops will have your best interests at heart?" Bee asked. "Look, I was a cop, and I know what it's like to work murders like this one. You go for the most parsimonious connection. The one that makes sense. You make sense. But I happen to know you're not the murdering type."

"Gee thanks."

"And I happen to know how to figure out who is." Bee lifted her head, a smile flashing across her lips, revealing the gap between her two front teeth.

My friend had already boarded the 'free Ruby' bus, even though I wasn't technically in trouble yet.

"Let's just take it easy, Bee. I know you're keen to investigate," I said—it had to be difficult for her to put that life aside. "But we don't want to get involved. We're trying to sell cookies not get involved in the inner workings of a town."

"Didn't you say that Harper woman mentioned the mayor? That Misty was the mayor's daughter?" Bee asked.

I nodded.

"Oh boy. This is going to escalate quickly. They'll want to close this case as soon as possible."

Before I could say anything, footsteps approached, and a detective appeared next to our bench. He was tall, balding, with a gray fringe of hair around his head. He stared down at us over a hooked nose. He was tan and almost... leathery.

A tough nut to crack.

"Good afternoon, ladies, my name is Detective Wilkes," he said.

I got up and put out my hand. "Ruby Holmes."

"You were the one who found her?"

"Yes, sir," I said.

Chatter interrupted our conversation, and I searched for the source—a group of people had gathered across the road. Some locals with a reverend standing among them, wearing his black clerical shirt and tab. My stomach sank. Great. Now everyone knew we were involved. What would this mean for the food truck?

"And what about you, ma'am?" Wilkes asked, turning to Bee.

"I'm her friend," Bee said. "She called me after it happened for moral support."

"So you didn't witness anything yourself?"

"No, sir, I joined Ruby a while after y'all rolled up on the scene."

The detective nodded. "All right then. I'll need to borrow Miss. Holmes for a few moments to discuss what happened." His smile was sharp around the edges and filled with mistrust. Could I blame him? I'd found the mayor's daughter dead as a doornail. "Let's head down to the police station."

"Is that necessary?" Bee put in. "Surely, you two can just talk here?"

Wilkes' smile disappeared like it had been sucked into the center of a black hole. "No. She'll have to come with me."

"Is everything all right here, detective?" The reverend who'd been placating the crowd of onlookers had crossed the road in the interim and stood on the brick sidewalk outside the bakery. He peered inside the windows, but the body had already been taken away by folks in forensic gear.

The detective chewed on air for a second. "Pastor Byrne," he said. "Everything's under control. No need for you to check in."

"Oh, of course it's under control," the pastor, not reverend, said, his green eyes twinkling behind square-rimmed glasses. He was young, probably in his early thirties, with a head of chestnut-brown hair, and an easy grin on thin lips. "I wouldn't doubt you or your stellar officers for a second. But I saw you talking to these two ladies and wondered if they were all right. I wouldn't want new members of the flock to feel any type of way about what's happened here today."

"What do you know about what's happened here today, pastor?" Wilkes' asked. "I was under the impression that news hadn't yet reached the ears of the... flock."

I could almost hear the inverted commas Wilkes' had put around 'flock.' Clearly, there was no love lost between these two men.

"Oh, you know how things are here, detective," the pastor said, a slight Irish lilt slipping into his words. "News spreads fast in Muffin. I hear it was that poor Misty that was the victim, yes?"

"I'm not at liberty to disclose that information at this point," Wilkes' replied.

If this Pastor Byrne dude was at all worried about the cold reception, he didn't show it. Instead, he turned to us and spread his arms. "Lovely to meet you, ladies. My name is Pastor Jack Byrne. Only a pity we weren't introduced sooner." A slight dig at the detective? What was up with them? "I take it you're new to town?"

"Yes," I said. "I'm Ruby and this is Bee."

"A pleasure. A pleasure. Well, I hope you'll stop by the church this week if you're feeling low after all of this hoopla."

"Thank you," I replied.

Bee didn't say a word but sat watching Wilkes' through narrowed eyes.

"If you'll excuse us, pastor," the detective said. "Miss. Holmes? Follow me, please."

I had no choice but to do as he'd asked. The alternative would be refusing to cooperate, and that would make everything worse. "I'll meet you back at the inn," I said to Bee, then followed the detective to his car, trying to ignore the burning stares of the onlookers across the street.

Four

THE QUESTIONING AND STATEMENT-TAKING HAD lasted for the better part of two hours, but it was over at last, and I had taken an Uber back to the inn, the purple of early evening settling around my shoulders and the lovely building in front of me.

The Runaway Inn faced the road with white clapboard walls and a central cupola peeking out of its gabled roof, three stories up. The garden out front was empty thanks to the cold snap that had come with winter, but the trees and their spindly branches stretching to the sky made the inn seem cozier.

Perhaps, that was to do with the warm light spilling out of the glass panes of the front doors, and the windows either side of it. Cars were parked neatly in a row in their designated spaces on brick paving a few paces from the central path leading up to the steps—the food truck was one of them. A flagpole bearing the US flag stood proudly on the lawn.

It was the type of place that spoke of years of service and pride, and I loved it already.

"Ruby!" Bee bustled out onto the front porch.

"I'm back."

"Evidently." She rushed down the steps and toward me. "Don't worry, I've gotten us two rooms right next to each other. Not conjoining like last time, unfortunately, but I've had your things brought up."

"Thank you," I said, looping my arm through hers.

We walked up the garden path together, onto the front steps of the gorgeous building, and entered.

A portly, elderly woman sat behind the reception desk —a glossy, walnut affair—sipping from a dainty china teacup. She looked up and smiled at us. "Oh, hello, dear, you must be Ruby. Beatrice has told me so much about you. It's lovely to have you at the inn. Will you be staying for dinner?"

"Actually, we were hoping to head out to some local restaurants," I said, "and it's lovely to meet you too. Didn't catch your name?"

"Mrs. Rickleston," she replied. "A pleasure to have you here. I believe that's your food truck parked outside? I've had such a hankering for donuts lately. I'd love to try one of yours."

The donuts served to remind me about the murder, and I had to have paled because Mrs. Rickleston gave a start. "Are you all right, dear?"

"Fine, thank you. Just tired and hungry."

"You go get changed, Rubes," Bee said. "I've already got the restaurant picked out."

"Great!"

We headed up to the second floor, and Bee handed over my room key. I let myself into a lavender-themed bedroom with a double bed and a view of the street outside. It was tight, cozy, and cute in here, but I would miss the ease of access that had come with having an adjoining bathroom with Bee. After all, we'd spent a lot of late nights drinking hot chocolate and coming up with cupcake ideas and murder mystery theories together in Maine.

I took a quick shower, dressed for the night out in a pair of jeans and a fitted sweater, then met Bee downstairs.

"Are you ready to go?" Bee asked.

"Absolutely. Where are we going?"

Bee brought out her phone and showed me the directions she'd brought up to a restaurant called La Griglia. "Apparently, it's the best Italian food we'll ever eat."

"I'm excited," I said, clapping my gloved hands

together and rubbing them. It would be nice to get out after having sat in an interrogation room for hours. Doubtless, Bee and I would get to talking about what had happened to Misty and how. We didn't know enough to make assumptions yet.

We headed out in the food truck together and found the Italian restaurant, with its windows underneath green, red, and white striped overhangs, just around the corner from the inn. The inside of the restaurant was decorated with square tables, warm candlelight, and private cushy booths. Gentle Mediterranean music tinkled from speakers in the corners, and the walls were rough brick, completing the rustic effect.

"I love it here," I said, as we took our seats at a booth.

"It's comfy," Bee agreed.

The waiter arrived and offered us menus with a flourish, wiggling his thick dark eyebrows at me. "Here you go, signora," he said, his accent thick. "Let me know if you need anything at all. Something to wet the throats, perhaps?"

"Just a Shirley Temple for me," I said.

"I'll take a glass of wine." Bee shrugged. "Why not? We're in Italy tonight."

The waiter swept off again to put our orders in, and I sat back, smiling at the warmth and happiness that now enveloped us. My gaze drifted to the side, and I made eye contact with a pretty woman with dark curly hair, and a set of oversized glasses. She frowned at me.

What's that about?

The man seated across from her, also dark-haired, but bearing a few tattoos on the backs of his hands and up his arms, didn't look our way, but glared off in the other direction.

"Hmm," Bee said. "I'd wonder why she's staring at you, but I think I know."

"It's because of the murder, isn't it?" I focused on the menu instead of the staring woman. "Everyone thinks I had something to do with it."

"Doubtful," Bee replied. "I spoke to Mrs. Rickleston while you were with that detective. Apparently, Misty was as well-hated as you heard this morning. People couldn't stand her. She'd made several locals ill with her baked goods."

That didn't bode well for figuring out who'd killed her. *Wait, I'm not seriously considering getting involved in all of this again, am I?* Old habits died hard—as an ex-investigative journalist, I struggled to keep my curiosity under control.

"What else did she say?" I asked.

"That if anyone would've wanted to get rid of Misty, it would have been her sister," Bee whispered.

"Her sister." I didn't have siblings, but I couldn't

imagine wanting to hurt anyone in my family. Shoot, not that I could imagine hurting people outside of my family either.

"Olivia Murphy," Bee said, turning her head so that it faced the brick wall. "Apparently, they didn't get on well. And from what Mrs. Rickleston said, Olivia just so happens to have dark hair and wear oversized glasses."

I glanced over at the woman again. She'd given up on staring at me now and was instead sitting in awkward silence with the man across from her.

Was it her? Was she Olivia?

"Bee, did you know she would be here?" I asked.

"I swear, I didn't. Though, I'm flattered you think I could rustle up that kind of Intel on such short notice. I guess, everyone really likes this restaurant."

Before Bee could tell me more of what she'd found out, the smarmy waiter reappeared to take our order. I opened my menu. "I'll have the meatballs to start, please." They sounded delicious—bathed in a marinara sauce with a side of crusty bread.

"The grilled calamari with tartare sauce, please," Bee said.

"Of course." The waiter, Gino by his nametag, swept into a deep bow then hurried off again.

The smells in the restaurant—garlic, lemon, basil and melting cheese—were almost too much to take.

"I think we should find out more about the sister," Bee said, directing my attention away from the delicious food to come. "Namely, what types of problems she had with Misty."

It was tempting, and I brought my purple-leather backed journal from my purse and set it on the table. I opened to a new page and scrawled Misty's name across it.

"You know," Bee said, "you really should get a separate notebook for case work. Your journal is meant to be personal."

"It is," I replied. "But it's not like I plan on investigating many more cases." I tapped the end of my pen next to Misty's name then wrote down the suspected murder weapon and the place it had all gone down—the bakery.

The waiter returned with our dishes and presented them, and I quickly shut my diary.

"Is there anything else I can get for you lovely ladies?" Gino asked.

I caught his arm. "Could you tell us who those two people are?" I nodded as discretely as possible.

Gino glanced over and stiffened. "Those two?" He shook his head. "Her name is Olivia, beautiful, beautiful lady, but the man? Very dangerous. You must stay away from him."

"What's his name?" Bee asked.

"Thomas O'Leary," Gino whispered, and his upper lip

had actually gathered sweat. "Trust me. You don't want to know that man. He's the type who gets involved with... the wrong side of the law. Those types of people, if you know what it is I'm saying."

"Thank you."

We sat at the table and started our meal, but I'd already noted down his name in my journal. If this Thomas O'Leary wasn't to be trifled with, and he knew Olivia who was Misty's sister... the insinuation was there.

"I wonder what this week will hold," I said, as I cut into my juicy meatball.

Bee gave me the look. The 'let's investigate and get to the bottom of the murder' look, and, this time, I couldn't really complain. It might be my neck on the line if we didn't find out who'd done it.

Five

Getting information about where Olivia Murphy stayed was super easy. Mrs. Rickleston was a gossip extraordinaire, and the minute we'd told her we'd seen Olivia out last night, she'd started talking like we were detectives and she was a witness.

Olivia's home was gorgeous—a brick-faced construction behind a picket fence along a street full of similarly cozy homes in Muffin's version of suburbia. Bee and I stood outside the gate, a cold wind whipping around us.

Once again, I held a box from the Bite-sized Bakery in my hands. We'd prepared a selection of treats—cupcakes, donuts, and macarons. It was our way of sweetening the deal. And of getting Olivia to talk.

"Let's not go too hard," I said.

"What do you mean?"

"You know how you are, Bee."

"Hey, I know how to interrogate a suspect," she replied.

"Yes. Interrogate. But this isn't an interrogation. Let's try our best to be nice and tactful."

Bee chuckled. "I'm known for my tact."

"It's practically your middle name." But I was only teasing. Without Bee, we would never have solved the mysteries we'd had in the past, and the food truck certainly wouldn't have been as successful as it was now.

"Let's go," Bee said.

We entered and walked up the pathway to the front steps of the house. The brass knocker glinted in the sun. It would've looked inviting and homely if not for the tension in my neck.

I used the knocker, and Bee and I waited.

The latch clacked, the door opened, and the woman we'd been waiting to see appeared. Olivia Murphy was lovely, but had dark circles under her eyes—they weren't bloodshot, though, and it didn't seem as if she'd been crying.

"Can I help you?" Olivia asked, her gaze falling to the box in my hands. "Oh, no, thank you. I'm not buying anything, thanks." She made to close the door.

Bee was quick as a flash. She pressed her palm to the

wood. "We're not selling anything," she said. "We came to offer our condolences for your loss."

"My loss?" Olivia opened the door again. "What loss?"

"Misty," I said. "I, uh, I was the one who found her."

"Oh!" Olivia nodded. "Oh right, yeah."

"Here." I foisted the box on her.

"Thank you," she said. "That's thoughtful of you. I don't recognize you from around town?"

"We're new," I replied. "We work on the food truck?"

"Oh right, I heard about that place. Misty flipped out about it yesterday afternoon." Olivia rolled her eyes, and then they widened as if she'd just realized what she'd said. She'd put herself near her sister on the day of the murder. And she wasn't upset about her passing at all. "Anyway, that's great that you're here. I'm sure it will, uh, be great for your business."

"Yeah, we hope so. Unfortunately, it seemed that your sister wasn't our biggest fan," I said.

"Oh, of course she wasn't. Misty was threatened by anyone who had a talent for baking." Another eye-roll from Olivia. "At least, no one has to deal with her drama anymore. She caused so much of it."

Yeah, there wasn't a tear in sight here. "She did?"

"Oh yeah." Olivia looked nothing like her sister. She was skinny, tall, and with dark hair and eyes, and a tan too.

Whereas Misty had been pale, blue-eyed, and furious. "I'm not surprised someone finally killed her."

"What?"

"Seriously," Olivia continued, shrugging her shoulders. "I wanna pretend that it's a shock and that I miss her, but me and my sister, well, we just didn't get along that well. That's all there is to it."

"Oh."

"Yeah, she was mean, and she had nothing good to say about anyone. She took our parents' bakery and drove it into the ground with poor management and bad customer service. But you know what?" Olivia drew in a breath. "None of that matters anymore. It's fine. Thanks for coming by." She retreated into the house and shut the door in our faces, taking the treats with her.

Bee sniffed. "Well, there's our answer."

"Sort of," I said.

We hurried back to the sidewalk and continued down it. I couldn't help glancing back at the beautiful home. I could've sworn the curtains in the window had twitched as if someone had been looking out, watching us walk away.

"What do you make of it?" I asked.

"That Olivia had a reason to get rid of her sister."

"Maybe that man she was with last night had something to do with it."

"I agree," Bee said. "It's time we found out more about

him. Maybe, I should put in a call to a few of my friends in high places." Bee had been a police officer in her time, and I didn't doubt she had contacts if she said she did.

"Friends in this state?"

"Oh yeah. Don't worry, Ruby, we'll get to the bottom of this."

I cast one final glance back at the house.

Six

After a full day on the food truck, and our interlude with Olivia, who clearly didn't care much about her sister's death, I was bone-tired. The food at the Runaway Inn was fantastic, though, and was a balm for all that ailed me.

"I hope you enjoy it, dear." Mrs. Rickleston stood near the entrance to the dining room, watching with a hawk-eyed glare as her helpers streamed past and set out plates of food in front of the guests.

The inn was full-up, as were all the tables—there were businessmen and women, a young family with two kids, and elderly and young couples, all seated at the circular tables, polished to a sheen and shining beneath the light of the bronze chandeliers.

The curtains were held back by thick cream sashes,

providing a view of the sidewalk and the wrought-iron lamps on the street outside. It was so gorgeous here that I couldn't help staring at the view. It helped me relax.

"I'm starved," Bee said, and picked up her knife and fork.

Tonight, we'd both selected the hot clam chowder with bread sticks and butter on the side. I ate it greedily, spooning it into my mouth as if I'd never eaten before. "So good," I said.

"Isn't it?" Bee took a sip of her water. "I'm glad we decided to come here."

"Me too. Kind of. I'm happy about the town," I said, "but not about what I walked in on the other day." I kept my voice low, checking that the other guests hadn't heard. They were out-of-towners too, and they likely wouldn't be listening in but still.

"That reminds me," Bee said, and dabbed her lips. She brought out her cellphone and set it on the table. "We have some research to do."

"What, here?"

"Why not?" Bee asked. "No one's watching us."

"I guess..."

Bee finished off the last spoon of her chowder then shifted her chair around so we were seated next to each other. She unlocked her phone. "All right." She opened a browser tab while I glanced around at the other tables, already paranoid.

Which was silly, if I considered it—I'd never been shy about researching things in Carmel Springs.

Bee typed 'Thomas O'Leary' into the search bar, and the results populated instantly. And boy, were there a lot of them. Thomas' mugshot was online, along with newspaper articles decrying him as a member of the Irish mob.

"Whoa."

"That's what I'm thinking." Bee opened up one of the articles, dated a few months prior, and the headline came up bold.

The Last Spider: Ex-Conman Turned Good Insists He Wasn't Involved in Fire

I read and re-read the title. A spider? What did that mean? Bee and I fell silent as we read.

Arrested last week on suspicion of arson, Thomas O'Leary, ex-Somerville Spider who turned on others in his organization, was insistent that he had nothing to do with the fire that took hold of Little Mama's Bakery in Boston last weekend.

"The fact that I'm out here, talking to you about this, well, that's all that needs to be said. They got nothing to hold me on, so that's why I can give interviews. What can I say? What can I say?" Thomas spoke with one of our representatives on

the phone, Monday. "They think that they can pin this on me because, really, they want to put me away. They want it so that they can get rid of me because I'm a problem for them."

Mr. O'Leary refused to expand upon those final comments, though, insisting that he was innocent and that it would be proven when the real arsonist was nabbed.

"Wow." I sat back. "That can't be a coincidence."

"What are these Somerville Spiders?" Bee whispered and tabbed back to the search bar. She typed in the name of the group and another series of articles popped up. "Well, well, well."

"What?" I pushed my clam chowder dish to one side. "What does it say?"

"Apparently, the Somerville Spiders are a now defunct mob that operated out of Beacon Hill. Dangerous—racketeering, human trafficking, drugs, alcohol, you name it. They did it."

"Oh no," I whispered.

"Oh no, indeed."

"And the article mentioned that Thomas had been arrested for arson," I said.

Bee nodded, sagely.

"At a bakery."

"Interesting that Olivia, who hated her sister, would be hanging around with a man like that," Bee said.

I opened my mouth to expand on that, but Mrs. Rickleston arrived at the table, smiling. "Did you enjoy your meals, dears?" she asked. "Did you have enough?"

"Yes, thank you," I said. "It was delicious. Best meal I've had since I arrived."

"Oh, that's wonderful." Mrs. Rickleston collected our plates. "Don't go anywhere just yet, I've got some delicious apple cider donuts on the menu, served with a custard ice-cream."

"Yum."

Our host swept the dishes away, and another waiter appeared to refill our water glasses and bring us coffees or teas—whatever our hearts desired. Mrs. Rickleston's inn was definitely bigger than Sam's had been back in Carmel Springs, and she ran it differently, but it was homely in its own way.

Apart from the fact that there was a murderer on the loose, and that our suspect list had just doubled. Olivia had hated her sister, and she had an ex-mob man friend, one who'd potentially burned down a bakery in Boston.

"What do you think?" I asked. "What do we do?"

"Hmm." Bee tapped her chin. "I'm not sure there's much we can do yet. We can keep an eye out for rumors and information for now."

"On the truck," I agreed. This way we could focus on the real reason we'd come to Muffin—it wasn't to investigate murders. Good heavens, at this rate, I'd never escape that horrible feeling of judgment that experienced in New York. My thoughts turned to my ex-fiancé, Daniel, who had disappeared on me, and my mood dropped.

"Here we are, ladies." Mrs. Rickleston had reappeared with two plates—an apple cider donut sat atop each with a ramekin of ice-cream beside it. "Enjoy."

"Thank you." How could I possibly be unhappy when there was so much to be grateful for? I had a friend who I traveled and baked with, great food to eat, a small town to explore, and now, another mystery to solve. I didn't like to admit it, but I missed my old job in a way—there had been plenty of intrigue, and I'd enjoyed uncovering the truth.

And Muffin had many secrets waiting to be uncovered.

Seven

THE LAST TIME WE'D WOUND UP INVOLVED IN A murder investigation, through no fault of our own—unless I counted walking in on a dead body—our food truck had suffered. People had decided that I was a femme fatale or a woman who'd poison my customers. The truck had done terribly, and Bee and I had contemplated leaving the town altogether.

But in Muffin? Folks weren't that worried about whether we'd poison them or not. The truck had never done better.

Two lines spread from the front window and wound onto the path that ran alongside the duck pond. Gossip was rife, with everyone from the elderly to adolescents whispering, chattering, talking behind their hands.

"Good morning," I said, trying for cheerfulness,

though I'd been asked about a million times whether I'd killed Misty. Most of the people who'd asked had framed it in a thankful tone. Or had even said that whoever had gotten rid of her, while it was terrifying there was a murderer on the loose, had 'done the town a favor.' I'd never come across a more detested woman. "Hello?" I peered at the customer standing first in line.

A young man wearing an ascot and his hair in blonde waves. "Good morning," he said, flopping his fringe back from his eyes. "Yeah, I just wanted to ask if you'd heard anything from that Detective Wilkes?"

"No," I said, stiffly, "I haven't."

Bee handed over a box to the customer at the front of her line. "And for the last time," she said, "I don't know anything about the murder. Neither does Ruby."

It had been the same for her all morning. We'd barely gotten a second to catch our breaths between questions.

"So," my customer prompted, "you don't know anything yet? Like, he hasn't told you whether you're a person of interest?"

"Sir, would you like to order something?" I kept my tone calm though my frustration bubbled away beneath the surface. "We have a vast selection of treats for every palette. This week's donuts are particularly good."

"Is that why you did it?" the guy asked. "Because, if that's the case, I totally get it. I mean, it's scary, but I can totally see this being some type of…"—he waved a hand at me— "baker's quarrel or whatever."

"There was no baker's quarrel. I simply found Misty. That's all there is to the story. Now, can I get you anything to eat?"

"Yeah, I'll take one of those cupcakes, please." He tapped on the glass case, pointing to the glistening lemon meringue cupcakes we'd made this morning.

"Sure. Coming right up." I packaged the cupcake as quickly as possible, handed it over, and accepted his money. I'd never been happier to see the back of a customer.

But then the next one in line stepped forward, and the questioning started again. It continued that way for the following five customers, and when another came forward and halted in front of my counter, I was just about ready to bite someone's head off.

"Good morning," said the woman, who had dark hair with purple streaks in it. "I bet you're tired of talking about Misty."

"Not so much talking about it," I replied, pleasantly surprised by her demeanor. "More frustrated at having to answer questions about it, I'd say."

"I'm sorry about that. People in Muffin are pretty inquisitive. Or nosy. Whichever works for you."

Bee snorted beside me.

"They mean well," the woman said. "I'm Lucy, by the way. Lucy Cornwall. I work over at Hashtag Nailed It, the salon? You should come by some time."

"It's lovely to meet you." We shook hands over the counter. Lucy's fingers were tipped in long magenta claws, and she bore an unnaturally dark tan.

"And you," I replied. "What can I get for you?"

"I'll take two strawberry glazed donuts, please."

"Sure!" I set about bringing them out of their case and placing them in a box.

"Don't worry about all of these people," Lucy said, gesturing to the other customers. "They're just curious because they got nothing going on in their lives. Besides, every one of 'em hated Misty with a passion."

I didn't know what to say, so I opted for silence.

"If you want the honest truth from me, though?" Lucy paused, clicking her nails together. "I don't think it was either of you two."

"You don't?" It was a refreshing perspective.

"No, I don't. And I got a reason too." Lucy licked her lips. And, somehow, the purple-pink gloss slathered across them didn't budge. She leaned closer. "Because I saw Misty get into a fight with someone yesterday morning. Right in front of her bakery." She let that linger in the air for a minute. "And I'm not talking like... a verbal altercation neither. I'm talking like... there were fists flying and everything."

"Who did you see?" I asked.

"Misty and that artist. The rich lady. Harper Kelly, that's her name. Blonde and real pretty, but she's got a temper on her, I'll tell ya that much."

"You're sure?"

"Oh yeah."

I handed Lucy her box, accepted the money then handed over her change. "Thank you. I hope you'll stop by again."

"Oh, I for sure will," Lucy said. "Listen, just don't take what any of these people say to heart. They all got their own issues, know what I'm saying?" She flounced off with her box, her hair bouncing.

"Did you hear that?" I grabbed a soda from the fridge behind Bee and cracked it open. I took a sip and set it to one side. Even the owner had to have a drink now and again.

"I heard. Very interesting. Wasn't Harper the one who first told you about Misty's bakery?"

"She was."

Before we could talk more, another customer stepped up, and another. The morning rush in Muffin was no less intense than it had been in Carmel Springs. People wanted their sweet treats and fixes, and they wanted them *now*.

The path that led into the park filled with people, and I barely had a minute to catch my breath, let alone take another sip of soda. Not that I was complaining. But what Lucy had said had set off a chain reaction of suspicion and curiosity. What exactly had Harper and Misty been fighting about?

We'd have to find out.

Finally, the morning rush dulled, and there was that idyllic quiet before brunch struck. I grabbed a muffin and headed out of the truck then took a seat on one of the benches to enjoy it. Bee and I took our breaks in shifts, just in case someone showed up and needed assistance.

I admired the view. The duck pond stretched out in front of me, the grassy green of the park spreading between trees on the other side, and on the hill further up behind it, sat the open gates of the stone church with its gorgeous steeple. It had to have been around when the town was first formed.

Two people exited the church's open doors, a young woman in a crimson dress, and a man—the pastor who we'd run into the other day. They spoke, though I couldn't really make anything out in the distance. And the woman raised a hand. A shout rang out, then faded. She spun away from the pastor and charged out of the gates, taking a left onto the street past the park, and soon disappeared behind the tree line.

What on earth had that been about?

"Ruby," Bee called from the food truck.

I finished off my food, disposed of everything neatly in a trash can, then hurried back to join her for the brunch rush, setting aside the woman in the red dress for later. After all, we didn't have to uncover all of Muffin's secrets. Just the ones that proved I hadn't killed Misty Murphy.

Eight

HARPER KELLY WASN'T JUST RICH, SHE WAS 'OWN an art gallery' rich. That art gallery was right on Gallop Road, its glass doors open to the public, and its walls festooned with pictures that I guessed she had painted? I wasn't a great judge of art, but they weren't the Mona Lisa, that was for sure.

Fruity classical music tinkled through the speakers, and we had been given a glass of sparkling grape juice in a champagne flute at the door. Bee held hers to her lips, her head tilted to one side, one eye narrowed.

"I don't get it," she said. "Maybe I'm just tired?" We had come to the gallery after closing the food truck. The last vestiges of the afternoon hovered around the horizon in bursts of pink and orange.

"I don't think you're meant to get it, to be fair." I took

a sip of my now tepid grape juice and tried not to grimace. I'd shrugged off my apron back on the truck, but I still had a couple splotches of sugar and jam and sticky glaze on my sweater and jeans.

"Good, because I don't understand this at all." Bee turned around and scanned the inside of the gallery. There were a few people milling around, checking the place out, but it was mostly empty. That might've been because most folks had already gone home or were eating at the rowdy bar and grill next door.

"Do you see her anywhere?" Bee asked. "I can't remember what she looks like. I didn't talk to her face-to-face."

"Not yet." I walked a little further along, pretending to admire the sculptures and pictures, but I kept searching for our target. *Target? Good heavens.* But that was what she was, now. We needed answers!

I gripped my journal under one arm, thinking of the case notes that needed to be made and the connections that were missing.

Thankfully, it seemed that Detective Wilkes wasn't quite as obsessive as the detective in Carmel Springs had been, but that didn't mean we'd rest on our laurels and forget about the entire investigation.

The music tinkled on, we slurped on our warm grape juice and crossed a barrier between exhibits. The black and white from before turned to yellow and blue, shades that made my eyes water.

"Good heavens," Bee said, dabbing at the corners of her eyes with her pinky fingers. "That's quite something."

"You like it?" A woman spoke from next to one of the paintings.

I yelped and spilled grape juice on my sweater. Bee didn't react except to inhale.

"Oh, did I startle you?" Harper Kelly offered us a smile each. It was no wonder I hadn't seen her standing there. She'd dressed herself in shades of yellow and blue that matched the paintings, and she wore heavy, pendulous sapphire earrings that tugged on her earlobes.

"No," Bee said, "she usually does this. It's her form of art."

I bit back a laugh, but it soured at the thought of getting the grape juice out of my sweater.

"To each their own," Harper said, airily, her gaze darting to my diary in hand and back up to my face. "It's wonderful to see you again, Trudy."

"Ruby," I said. "It's Ruby."

"Of course. I apologize." Harper's pleasant demeanor was similar to the one she'd had the other day, but now she'd put on airs and graces. Like she was the Queen rather than a gallery owner. "What brings you here today?"

"Just thought we'd see some sights Muffin has to offer," I replied.

"And we wanted to wash our eyes out," Bee put in. "Sort of like cutting an onion, isn't it?"

Harper frowned.

I cleared my throat to distract her. "It's a lovely exhibit. Did you do it all yourself?"

"Most of it," Harper said, raising her head. "I do source some outside art from local artists. You know, just to support them." She shrugged as if it was nothing. "I'm glad you stopped by, though. I can tell you about the pieces. You see, I take my inspiration from the greatest artist to walk the face of the Earth. Pablo Picasso. My favorite."

"That's... nice." I tried searching for a resemblance, but saw none. Then again, I wasn't an art buff.

"Are you interested in buying?" Harper raised an eyebrow.

"Buying?" Bee asked. "Another glass of champagne?"

"No, a piece of art of course, you silly goose." Harper tittered at the joke.

"We were just stopping by before we head over to grab something to eat," I said, searching for the right segue. "Been working on the truck all day. Funny thing, though, we ran into someone who mentioned that you and Misty got into a fistfight. We just wanted to check that you were OK."

"Me? I'm fine," Harper said, tossing her hair. "But why are you asking?"

"Oh, we just heard a rumor," I replied. "And from our talk the other day, it got me worried that maybe you might have seen something. You know, if you and Misty got into a fight, you might have passed the murderer in the street." I made my eyes wide, as if the thought haunted me.

"Goodness, no. I didn't see anything, thankfully. I spoke to Misty during the morning, though it wasn't really speaking and more shouting. You see," Harper said, tapping her fingernails against her cheek, "everyone in Muffin knows I'm wealthy, including Misty, and she's not. She'd run through all her funds, and her father refused to give her any more. So, she tried to get me to give her money. I refused. She threw a punch. I extracted myself from the situation."

"Wow." I wasn't sure I'd bought a word of it. Except for, perhaps, that Misty had wanted money from Harper.

"We weren't the best of friends, that's for sure. But then, no one in town liked Misty. She was a horrible witch. She would do whatever she wanted to get ahead, and if you got in her way, well, she'd just try to get rid of you."

"Seems like someone decided to get rid of her instead," Bee said, pointedly.

Harper didn't register that it had been a jab. "Unfortunate. I guess." She pulled a face. "For Misty and her family. Her father came back from vacation when he heard."

"How sad," I said. "Well, it's good that you didn't see anything. If you had, the murderer might've come after you next."

Harper laughed. "Oh no. That wouldn't happen."

"Why not?" Bee asked.

"Because it just wouldn't, trust me."

"Harper, darling." A woman with a British accent waved from the front of the gallery.

"Excuse me. This is one of my clients. Feel free to enjoy the snacks and juice." She swept off, and I watched her leave.

"What do you think?" I asked.

"That Harper's a little too confident for her own good," Bee said, and pinched the bridge of her nose. "Also, she likes primary colors too much."

"Let's get out of here. We need to consolidate what we've found." And we had to prepare for something else. Or rather, I had to prepare for it. Tomorrow was Bee's birthday—she'd tried hiding it from me, but I'd managed to find out by a few choice online searches and phone calls. My investigative history had paid off again.

We hurried from the gallery, and I could've sworn that Harper's gaze had followed us.

Nine

The following morning

"WHAT'S GOING ON?" BEE ASKED, TEARING HER sleep mask down. "Why are you—?" She gasped, her fingers fluttering to her lips. "Are you serious? Ruby, I—how? How did you know?"

"I have my sources," I replied, from the foot of her bed. My arms were laden with gifts, and I grinned at her. "Since we didn't get to stay with Sam for your birthday, I figured I'd buy extra presents to make up for it."

"You shouldn't have done that." Bee pushed herself upright, but she couldn't hide her excitement.

Bee and I were so different but similar too. I doubted

she'd celebrated many of her past birthdays, and she definitely hadn't had friends to celebrate with.

I dropped the presents onto her bed, and she scooched up, eying them with thinly concealed glee. "This is all too much. Ruby... I mean—"

"Hey, remember my birthday? At least, I didn't organize a surprise party for you." I had to withhold a shudder. My party hadn't exactly gone to plan.

"That alone is a gift."

"Ha. Oh it wasn't that bad."

"There was a dead body strewn across the table," Bee said. "It was pretty bad."

I shivered again. "Anyway, I thought we'd take the day off the truck. We've done so well in sales this past week, we can afford it. And I doubt our customer-base will disappear. People are obsessed with what happened to Misty. More so than we are."

"I doubt that," Bee said, and unwrapped one of her gifts. A selection of baking-themed pins fell out—a cupcake, a donut, and a macaron. "These are adorable." She pinned one of them to her PJ top.

"I'm glad you like them. Since we're taking the day off, I thought we'd head out to the park and have a picnic lunch. Mrs. Rickleston was kind enough to pack a basket. We'll have some donuts and treats and go over what we have for the case."

"Yes," Bee hissed.

It was the best gift I could've given her, honestly. She missed working as a detective, and when things like this just fell into her lap, it was the obvious choice. Besides, we'd already peeled back a few layers of intrigue—Misty had been hated by Olivia, who had been seen with an ex-mob guy, and then there was Harper, who'd had an altercation with her.

"All right, you unwrap the rest of these," I said, giving her a hug. "Happy Birthday." Like me, I doubted Bee would appreciate the scrutiny while she opened her gifts.

"I'll meet you downstairs in twenty," Bee said, happily. "Thanks so much. Like I said, you didn't have to do this."

"What are friends for?"

Downstairs, I gathered everything for our picnic and checked the weather forecast on my phone. It would be sunny with a chill wind, but we'd survive. Besides, there were plenty of covered areas in the park, gazebos and the like, and exploring the town was a big part of our stay here. When I'd decided to get into the roaming food truck business, it had been to get away from New York and the memories and stares after Daniel had left me. But it had also been for the sense of adventure.

What was the point of stopping in gorgeous small towns across the country if we weren't going to explore them?

"Here you go, dear." Mrs. Rickleston handed me a wicker basket. "If there's anything else I can help you with, you just let me know."

"I will, thank you, Mrs. Rickleston."

She patted me on the cheek and squeeze it lightly. "Such a precious girl. You'll go far, you know. I can just tell, you're one of those women who have what it takes to succeed." And then she shuffled off again, heading for the swinging kitchen doors at the end of the dining area.

I didn't want to examine too closely what she'd said. Perhaps, because I didn't believe it of myself. Our trip thus far had been amazing but fraught with mistakes, failures and flops. Not in the baking department, though. Bee had that covered.

Oh stop it. Today will be a good day.

I set the basket on a sideboard then grabbed my box of glazed donuts and put them inside. I couldn't wait to find out what Mrs. Rickleston had packed for us. Her chef was a genius.

"Ready!" Bee presented herself at the base of the stairs, grinning and wearing her donut pin and a thick orange sweater, a trench coat and a pair of gloves.

"Great." We made our way out of the inn and down the road, opting for a brisk walk instead of a drive so we could take full advantage of the town's sights and sounds.

My cheeks iced up, but I didn't care. The sun was out,

cars trundled down the roads, and Muffin showed its beautiful side—the brick pathways, the shop windows, the men and women coming out to grab coffees at a local diner, laughing, chatting, joking.

"It's weird to think that this place has secrets," I said, softly.

"Every town has its secrets, Ruby," Bee said. "It just depends how deeply their hidden."

We reached the park and passed the duck pond where we usually parked. There were a few stragglers who perked up at the sight of us, but wrinkled their noses when they realized we wouldn't be setting up shop today.

Five minutes later, we had our seat under a gazebo and a blanket each over our laps. I rubbed my hands together and opened the picnic basket. Tempting scents drifted up to greet us. I removed the donut box then gaped at what was underneath it.

"Oh my heavens," I said. "Wow. Mrs. Rickleston outdid herself. Look at this. There are lobster rolls and roasted potato wedges, bacon sandwiches too."

"Let's hope none of it's poisoned," Bee said.

"That's not funny." But I laughed anyway. We took out all the treats and stacked the Tupperware boxes on the bench either side of us.

The lobster rolls were over-the-top delicious, and we ate them greedily, talking about Carmel Springs and how much we missed Sam and Millie and all the other folks there. The view filled me with joy too.

It was sad to miss our friends, and weird to be embroiled in another murder investigation, but I was happy.

"Ruby," Bee said, lowering her voice. "Is that Olivia Murphy?"

I followed her line of sight.

A couple walked across the grass together, heading for another of the gazebos nearby, hand-in-hand. The woman's hair was dark, but I couldn't make out whether it was Olivia from behind. But the man... he had tattoos down his arms just like Thomas O'Leary.

"I bet it is," I said. "And she's with that mob dude again."

"O'Leary."

"Right."

"Holding hands. Looks like Olivia had all the resources she needed to get rid of her sister. My question is why the police haven't arrested either of them if they did do it."

That was a question we'd have to get an answer for. After the lobster rolls, of course. "I think I know who we could ask about them."

Ten

The last information I'd received from Lucy, the nail technician who'd come to the truck, had been valid. And there wasn't a place that bred gossip better than a salon and all its inhabitants.

"Are we really doing this?" Bee asked, checking her nails.

"Oh, come on. It will be fun. How long has it been since you've had your nails done?"

"I don't remember."

"Exactly. This will be great. And we'll get some information out of it too. Besides, it's the perfect way to celebrate your birthday."

The outside of the Hashtag Nailed It salon stood out like a sore thumb. Most of the buildings in the street were brick-faced and humble, with flowerbeds under their windows and cheery fabric awnings. The salon, however, had been painted a violent shade of purple and slashed with zebra stripes of black, and its sign had been done in sparkling glitter.

"Oh no," Bee said, as we stopped outside it. "You've got to be kidding me."

"Do you want to find out what O'Leary and Olivia were doing together or not?" I asked.

A beat passed and then Bee sighed. "Fine. But my eyes are starting to water again. What is it with people in this town and bright colors?"

I pushed the glass front door open, and a merry chime rang through the interior—also styled in glittery purple and black.

"Oh hiya," Lucy waved from a table on the side of the room. Several nail stations were set up with chairs facing the technicians and most of them were occupied. Thankfully, Lucy's was free, and she rose from her seat and clip-clopped over in insanely high stilettos.

Lucy enveloped me in a perfumed hug. "Great to see you again, hon. Are you here to get your nails done?"

"No, we came to hammer up some drywall," Bee said.

Lucy guffawed. "You're funny. What's your name?"

Bee, who was used to her sarcastic humor being frowned upon, returned a gap-toothed grin. "Bee."

"Well, you can take seats right here." Lucy gestured to

her table and the one next to hers, where another glammed up technician sat inspecting her nails. The collection of fake nails not the ones on her fingers.

Bee took the seat in front of the technician we didn't know, and I took the comfy stool in front of Lucy's station. She lowered herself into place, tossing her hair back, her earrings and bracelets clattering noisily, and took a hold of my right hand.

"Let's see what we've got here." She examined my fingernails. "These cuticles need care."

"Yeah, I've been too busy for cuticle care."

"One should never be too busy for cuticle care, Ruby," Bee commented.

Lucy clicked her fingers and pointed them at Bee. "I like you. You've got a good head on your shoulders."

I cleared my throat. "I'd just like a manicure and, uh, French tips, please. That's it."

"Sure thing, baby doll." She set to work organizing her nail products then brought my fingers toward a warm bath of water.

I tried to relax, but it had been a long time since I'd had anyone touching me like this. And it kind of made me uncomfortable. *Don't be silly. This is meant to be fun.* It was also meant to be an information reconnaissance mission.

"So, what's new?" Lucy asked. "How's life in Muffin treatin' ya?"

"It was fine," I replied. "I mean, it is fine. I think I'm still a little shaken up after the murder."

"Of course, yeah, that's horrible. Can't imagine what that must've been like, walking in on somethin' like that? No thank you."

"Yeah," I said. "I spoke to Harper, by the way."

"Oh, you did? And what did *she* say? I bet she came over all snooty on you. She's like that. She thinks she can get away with..." Lucy raised her eyebrows. "Just because she's rich. But she hated Misty just like everybody else in town did. They don't even deny it."

"What about the people who Misty made sick?" I asked. "Did they ever get into fights with her?"

"Oh, probably. But she made a lot of people sick, so it's difficult to keep track."

"That many people?" I asked.

"Oh yeah, she even made her husband sick at one point."

"Ex-husband," the technician who had Bee's nails under her care said. "Tom ain't with her anymore."

"Tom?" I asked.

"Thomas O'Leary," Lucy replied. "He was Misty's man for years, but she was so crazy, she chased him away.

And he was not the kind of guy you messed with, if you catch my meaning. It's crazy how much he let her get away with. From what I heard, she had an affair."

"Tom and Misty were married?" My jaw dropped.

"Why so shocked?"

"We were in the park this morning and we saw Tom and Olivia together. Holding hands," I said.

Lucy released my hand, clapping hers to her cheeks. "No. Really?"

"Really," I said.

"They looked cozy?"

"Very cozy," I replied. "And we saw them at La Griglia the other night, as well."

Lucy brought my nails back into her care with a conspiratorial spy. "Now, that is something. I wonder how long that's been going on. I doubt Misty would've been happy about them being together."

"Do you think they were having an affair when Misty was still married to him?" the other nail tech asked.

"Hmm, I wouldn't put it past Olivia," Lucy said. "She hated her sister. You know, she was adopted before Misty was born, so they never really saw eye-to-eye. Because she was, like, older or whatever."

The new information practically rattled around the inside of my skull.

"I wonder if she'll be there at the funeral tomorrow," Lucy said.

"Misty's funeral is tomorrow?"

"That's right. At the cemetery behind the church. Though, I doubt anyone will be there." Lucy shrugged.

I glanced over at Bee. She gave me an infinitesimal nod. We had our next lead.

Eleven

BEE HAD CHOSEN A CLASSY OUTFIT—BLACK tailored pants, a black polo neck and a fleece black jacket to match. I had gone for a black trench with a maxi dress underneath because I didn't have that much black clothing.

Not that it mattered.

There were an awful lot of people wearing colorful clothing at Misty's funeral. It was scandalous. To make matters worse, there weren't many people in the cemetery present to pay their respects. There were a handful, apart from the pastor himself—the same man, Jack Byrne, we'd met in front of the bakery after Misty's death.

Other than him, the handful of guests intrigued me. Since everyone had, apparently, despised Misty, it made no sense that any of them would've been in attendance, unless they had agendas of their own.

"What do you think?" I asked, out of the corner of my mouth.

Pastor Jack held his bible in one hand, his eyes closed as he waxed lyrical about Misty's achievements. The coffin —a polished walnut behemoth—sat above its rectangle in the dirt, poised to be lowered inside.

"I think we probably shouldn't be talking while he is," Bee replied, also out of the side of her mouth.

"He's not praying. He's just talking about her." I frowned. "With his eyes closed."

"Emotional guy."

The pastor raised his hands. "As a child of the flock, Misty was dedicated. She believed that giving for the sake of giving would only wind up hurting those on the receiving end of those gifts. That it was important to teach a man to fish, rather than to give him food for a day."

I tried keeping my expression sorrowful, but it was difficult. Of course, it was Misty's funeral, so the pastor had to find something good to say about her—but couldn't he have done a little better than this?

The drone of his voice, caught halfway between sadness and concentration, crept between those gathered and the gravestones further back. A naked elm tree stood nearby, silent and watching. It didn't provide any shade, but it didn't need to today. The sky was gray.

Someone sneezed nearby, but there wasn't any sobbing.

I scanned the gathered people. Across from us, on the other side of the coffin and open patch of dirt, stood Olivia, her head bowed, but she was clothed in a cheery orange sweater. Next to her stood the wily-looking Tom O'Leary. They weren't holding hands this time.

Further back, nearer the elm tree, Harper Kelly hovered, tugging at the throat of her own polo-neck sweater in a shade of fuchsia. And that was it, apart from a woman I didn't recognize who hovered next to Pastor Byrne. She wore her hair dark, beneath a black hat, and was the only person dressed appropriately. Her gaze darted from left to right, constantly.

"Who do you think that is?" I whispered.

Bee hummed in her throat. "Must be the pastor's wife? Don't know who else would be here for Misty, dressed appropriately."

That was a good note. If she was the pastor's wife, we could probably exclude her from our sleuthing suspicions.

The pastor bowed his head in prayer, as did the shy woman to his right, but no one else did. Olivia glared at the coffin. Tom removed a pack of cigarettes from his pocket and lit up. He puffed on the end of his cigarette, blowing out clouds of smoke in what had to be a sign of extreme disrespect. Harper Kelly came forward, slowly.

She halted in front of the coffin, and the pastor stumbled over his words then continued, "—let us wish Misty farewell on her next great adventure in the sky."

What type of send-off is that? Adventure in the sky? I barely kept from shaking my head.

Baskets of rose petals had been placed around the coffin. None of the attendees came forward to lift them and toss the petals over the walnut top.

The coffin crank made a noise, and the walnut case lowered.

"Goodbye, Misty," Harper said, softly, tossing her hair back.

Olivia whipped around. "What did you just say?"

"Oh, hi, Olivia, I didn't see you there." Impossible, of course, since there were so few people here. "How are you holding up?"

The pastor remained where he was, studying the women. His wife tugged gently on his arm, but he ignored her.

"You didn't see me here?" Olivia scoffed. "Is that because you can't see anyone from up there on your high horse?"

"Pardon me?"

"You heard what I said," Olivia growled. "You need to leave."

Harper flushed red. "I'm here to pay my respects."

"No you aren't. You're here to rub salt in the wounds. Do you think I'm scared of you, Kelly? I know the truth. I know that you were the one who—"

"Ladies, please," Pastor Jack said, striding toward them, leaving his wife to trail after him. He laid a hand on each of their shoulders. "You must calm down. This is a funeral. We're here to bid Misty a fond farewell. If you need aid with conflict resolution, you're more than welcome to come back to the church and speak with me about this."

"All I need is for her to get out of here before I rip that fake blonde hair out of her head," Olivia snapped.

Tom took hold of her arm and muttered something I couldn't make out. She gritted her teeth but nodded, reluctantly. She took a step back then another, finally turned and strode away from the gravesite, her arms folded. Olivia talked to O'Leary, animatedly, but the wind carried her words in the opposite direction.

"Well," Pastor Jack said, making eye contact with me. "That was unfortunate. Are you all right, Miss. Holmes? Miss. Pine?"

"We're fine," Bee replied, evenly.

I looped my arm through hers, figuring it was time we

made our swift exit. We'd, kind of, got what we'd come for. More information. It appeared that Olivia was convinced Harper was up to something. She'd hinted at it when she'd said Harper was the one who'd... done what? Killed Misty?

"Let's go out to eat," Bee said. "We've got a lot to discuss."

I nodded, but cast one last glance over my shoulder at the lowering coffin and the small gathering around it. The pastor's wife was gone, and Jack stood with his arm around Harper's shoulders, nodding as she spoke quietly to him. They didn't notice me watching.

Was it just me, or was the pastor a little too familiar with some of his flock?

Twelve

Bee and I strode out of the restaurant, her clutching her coat closer and me impervious to the wind, only because I couldn't stop frowning about the whole 'funeral' issue.

It didn't make sense to me—why would Olivia have been so upset at Harper? If Harper had had something to do with Misty's death, Olivia surely wouldn't have cared? She had never liked her sister. She'd made that clear when we'd spoken to her.

"Well, at least the food was good," Bee said.

"You sound downright depressed."

"I'm always a little down when the leads on a case aren't going anywhere."

"You know," I said, "we have more important things to worry about. Like the truck. We can put all of this on hold if we want to. It's not like the police don't have it under control. It's not like we have to make it our life's pursuit."

"What do you mean? We just sit back and do nothing?"

"No, but we could, I don't know, keep an ear to the ground rather than being boots on the ground? Let's enjoy our time in Muffin instead of wasting it worrying about how well we're doing with figuring out who murdered Misty."

"I suppose," Bee huffed.

"Besides, we can head back to the truck and make some donuts."

"Now?"

We usually made our first batch fresh in the morning. "Yes, now," I replied. "Not for the customers tomorrow, but for us. What do you think?" Donuts, ironically, were Bee's soft spot. And she'd glare at me every time I made a 'cop-donut' joke.

"That's a great idea," Bee said, perking up. "We can do strawberry glazed again. I love strawberries. Pity they're not in season, right now."

We hadn't eaten any dessert—making donuts was the perfect way to unwind. Shoot, I'd already gained weight since I'd bought the food truck, but what was a woman to do? There were too many treats to deny.

Ten minutes later, we entered the street that held the

Runaway Inn, and approached the front of it, the decorative lampposts casting their circles of light along the sidewalk, guiding our path.

"Do you think that—?"

"Ruby." Bee tugged on my arm. "Ruby."

"What?" I'd been about to ask about tomorrow's specials.

"The truck."

We'd reached the front of the inn, and the cars parked out front were caught in gloom. The truck sat exactly where we'd left it, merry with its green and pink pastel stripes. The fabric awning that hung over the side window flapped gently in the wind, and the—

My eyes widened.

No. Not again!

The driver's side window had been shattered. Glass lay scattered on the tarmac. I rushed forward, Bee chasing after me, and brought my phone out of my handbag, directing the light from its screen inside the truck. The glove box had been yanked open and papers lay scattered over the passenger seat. The driver's side seat had been slashed with a knife and the stuffing poured out of it.

Anger clogged my throat. I forced myself to take a step back without touching anything.

"I'm calling the cops," Bee said.

What was it with small towns and theft? This had

happened to us in Carmel Springs too. I'd been so sure we'd left it all behind.

The more you interfere, the more dangerous things will get. The thought came about of nowhere, but it tickled my mind. I gasped.

"What?" Bee asked, her phone against her ear.

"My journal is missing," I said. "It was in the glove box."

"Oh?"

"It had all the notes we've been making about Misty in it."

DETECTIVE WILKES LISTENED PATIENTLY AS I repeated my suspicions for the third time. I'd insisted he take down notes while another police officer surveyed the scene and others took fingerprints.

"Ma'am, thank you for the information and suspicions, but until there's physical evidence tying someone to the scene, and that someone is also connected to the scene at the bakery, there's not much I can do but file this as a case of theft."

Frustration bubbled through me. "But you've got to understand, someone wanted that journal because it had my notes in it."

"Your notes?"

Bee had retreated into the inn to grab us both a cup of coffee after what had happened, and I was on my own here—doubtless, she'd be annoyed that I'd let anything slip. We'd found that most police officers didn't like it much when we interfered in their cases.

"Yes," I said, reluctantly.

"What notes?" Wilkes ran a leathery tan hand over his face. The man looked as if he'd been chewed up and spit out.

"Just, uh, a few things I picked up on serving folks on the food truck."

The detective stared at me.

I sighed. "You know, about Misty being hated by Olivia, and having had a fight with Harper Kelly. And the fact that Tom and Olivia are now a couple. That kind of stuff."

"Tom and Olivia," Detective Wilkes said, raising an eyebrow.

"Yeah."

"And you found out this information, how?"

"Like I said, just by being on the truck and around town. Why, have I told you something you didn't know? Is it about Tom?" I asked.

Wilkes ran a finger down his hooked nose, his gaze

unfocused now. "We're talking about the same Tom? Thomas O'Leary? Misty's ex-husband?"

"Yes." I had to take advantage of this unfocused expression. The detective still hadn't snapped back to reality. "Did Tom and Misty ever fight?" I asked. "You know, verbally or otherwise, while they were married?" Of course, every married couple had fights, but they were divorced and if Tom had a motive...

"A few reports," he said, under his breath.

"Domestic disputes?" I asked.

Detective Jones' head came up, and he focused on me, his eyes sharp and hawk-like. "Thank you for the information, Miss Holmes, but I suggest you stop writing notes about the case. We have this under control."

How could I believe that when I was still as suspect? And now, I knew for sure that I'd had information the detective hadn't. What was worse, my journal was gone—there had been more than just my case notes in there. Some criminal now had my private thoughts and feelings in their hands.

"Ruby?" Bee waved from the front step.

"You go on inside," the detective said. "We'll finish up out here and check in with you once we're done. I suggest you put a call in to your insurance company."

I thanked him, trying not to sound bitter, and headed up the path to the inn. Tomorrow, we wouldn't be able to go out and serve our delicious donuts and treats. The truck's window would have to be repaired, along with the seats.

Bee handed me a cup of coffee on the porch. "What do you say?" Bee asked. "Ready to get involved now?"

"With the case? You bet your bottom donut, I am."

"A bottom donut?" Bee asked. "That doesn't sound good. Sounds like something that would've been served in Misty's shop."

"That's it," I said, clicking my fingers and nearly losing my grip on the coffee cup. "We'll go back to the scene of the crime tomorrow."

"Or Misty's house. If there's going to be anything incriminating about O'Leary, it will be there," Bee said.

And with that, the pressure on my shoulders lifted a little—we had a plan. The last thing I wanted was a run-in with another murderer.

Thirteen

"THERE IS NOTHING BETTER THAN A STACK OF pancakes dripping in butter and syrup," Bee said, cutting into her pancake and lifting it to her lips. "Nothing." She ate the bite with relish, swirling the fork back and forth in front of her mouth.

"What about waffles?" I asked. "With ice cream and a cherry on top?" I cut into my omelet and ate a piece myself.

Mrs. Rickleston and her chef had outdone themselves for breakfast again. The Runaway Inn wasn't like Sam's guesthouse back in Maine. They had a menu here, whereas Sam had sort of prepared the meals and told us what we'd be getting.

I took a sip of orange juice. I was fortified by the food and the cozy atmosphere. It was early—well, early for most guests—at 8 am, and the dining area was empty. I shifted in my chair and peered out of the window at the poor food truck, waiting to be taken for repairs.

"So, the plan remains the same?" I asked.

Bee chewed on her pancake piece and swallowed, nodding. "First the bakery, then the house. Mrs. Rickleston has already divulged the address. The woman's a well-spring of gossip."

"Good thing we have her around to help us."

Bee dragged a slice of pancake through a pool of syrup. "Hmm. There's a problem with that, though. You just know she'll be gossiping about us too."

"She seems harmless enough."

"They all do," Bee said, "until the baker drops dead and we're prime suspects in the murder."

"Point taken."

I was both apprehensive and excited for the day to come. We'd been picking up bits and pieces of information here and there, but to go directly to the crime scene? Or to snoop around in Misty's house? That was a new level of investigating entirely.

One we'd partaken in before. And been punished for.

I finished off the last of my omelet and orange juice then dabbed with a napkin. Bee was still busy, so I filled the few minutes with a stare out of the window at the sun-filled street, the beginnings of early morning activity starting up across the road.

People got in their cars and drove off to work, or folks strode down the streets in their warm coats and woolen gloves.

"Miss Holmes?" Mrs. Rickleston had appeared next to our table.

"Yes?"

"Sorry to interrupt, dear, but I've just received this at the front desk for you. A young girl dropped it off." Mrs. Rickleston proffered a letter in a sealed envelope. My name was written in full in a long sweeping hand on the front.

"Oh, thanks." I accepted it from her and waited until she'd retreated to the reception area before turning to Bee. "That's weird. I haven't gotten an actual letter in ages. Who doesn't have email nowadays?"

"It doesn't have a stamp on it," Bee noted, putting down her fork and scooching her chair around to my side of the table. "Do you recognize the handwriting?"

"I don't think so." I turned the envelope open, but there was no return address on the back. Of course, there wasn't. It hadn't been sent by mail. A girl had dropped it off. How strange.

"Here." Bee grabbed her butter knife and handed it over.

I slit the top of the envelope with some effort then

turned it upside down and emptied the contents into my lap. A piece of folded paper fell out. I lifted it and opened it up.

Ruby,

It's been a while and this letter might come as a shock to you. I'm writing because you left me and I need the money you owe me. Meet me by the lake with the ducks tomorrow at noon.

Daniel.

The air in my lungs disappeared. Daniel? My ex, Daniel? The same man who had disappeared without a trace? Who had ghosted me? I blinked, trying to reread the words on the page, but they had turned into blurry squiggles.

"You're shaking," Bee said, extracting the letter from my grasp and reading it herself. She stiffened. "Is this supposed to be from…?"

"Yes. My ex."

"But—it says here that you left him?"

I shook my head. It didn't make sense. Was someone playing a trick on me? If so, it was cruel.

"And you didn't owe him any money, I assume?" Bee asked.

"Not at all. We kept our finances separate. He was the one who left, he was… gone one day. I only found out he was fine from his family, and even they were reluctant to talk about it. I don't know what happened or why, I—"

"It's OK." Bee squeezed my arm. "This is just another mystery for us to solve."

I stared at the letter, struggling to concentrate. Bee summoned a waiter and asked for a glass of soda to sweeten me up and chase off the shock. But I wasn't sure anything would do that.

Either someone had found my weakness and decided to play a cruel trick on me, or Daniel was back.

Fourteen

THE SHOCK HAD FINALLY WORN OFF AFTER A helping of Mrs. Rickleston's delicious pancakes. "It can't be Daniel," I said, as I set my knife and fork down. "It doesn't make any sense. Why would he have disappeared, broken our engagement and my heart, only to find me in a small town in Massachusetts?"

"I agree." Bee dabbed her lips with her napkin—she'd had a second helping of pancakes. She picked up the letter and flipped it open, scanning the contents again. "But who would have this type of information about you?"

"Mrs. Rickleston mentioned a girl had dropped it off. Maybe, if we find her, we'll have a lead."

"You don't think a young girl wrote this."

"No, of course not," I said, "but whoever did probably

paid her to drop off the letter. Since Mrs. Rickleston knows everyone, they can't risk doing it themselves."

"What about this meeting?" Bee closed the letter and slid it back into the envelope. "Do you want to go?"

"I'm not sure."

I rested my chin in my palm and peered out at the street again. The sun had risen higher, cars drove by, and I scanned the people walking outside. Muffin's atmosphere was so charming, but who knew what lurked beneath the surface.

I had a right to be paranoid this time.

"It seems like a trap," Bee said. "Someone's trying to get you to show your face."

"The murderer?" I asked.

"Maybe. It would make sense that whoever it was didn't want you snooping around town. And the truck has just been broken into."

"My journal was stolen." The cold sweep of realization washed over me.

"Then that's how they must have found out. They're using it against you."

Strangely, I had nothing but relief for that concept. The last thing I wanted was to run into Daniel again. I wasn't ready to confront that part of my past. It was the reason I'd left New York in the first place. So I wouldn't have to deal with the stares and the whispers and the potential confrontation that might amount from it.

"Then it's definitely a trap," I said. "I'd be interested to go, but I don't want to be stupid."

"Yeah, walking into a murderer's snare isn't exactly on my bucket list." Bee handed me the envelope and I tucked it into my handbag to keep as evidence.

"Then the plan remains the same for now," I said. "We head out to the crime scene and Misty's house, and we take it from there. Maybe we'll find some evidence that incriminates someone. And then we can give that to the police and go to this meeting tomorrow with 'Daniel.' What do you think?"

A gleeful, gap-toothed grin appeared on Bee's face. "Let's do this."

GOING BACK TO THE BAKERY HAD TURNED OUT TO be a terrible idea. The place was locked with a police department seal still on the front door. Cupping our hands and placing them to the glass had only provided us with a darkened glimpse of the bakery's grubby linoleum and the empty counters.

But that failure was behind us now.

I followed in Bee's footsteps as we darted along the fence that bordered Misty's property. Or it had been her property. Who knew what had happened afterward. Had Olivia gotten everything? Or perhaps it had been her ex-husband, Tom?

That would've explained why they were so cozy, now.

It was late afternoon, but the house next-door to Misty's was empty, missing its curtains and its window panes covered in a layer of dust. Misty's home was brick and set back from the road behind a high fence. The side fence, however, the one we stalked along, wasn't as tall.

The flowerbeds under Misty's windows were completely empty, and she had no porch to speak of. A selection of empty bottles sat outside the front door—not milk, but wine, champagne and beer. A broken wind chime spun in circles under the eaves, clacking noisily.

"Creepy," I whispered.

"Agreed. Now, let's get over this fence without anyone getting suspicious."

"No offense, but we look pretty suspicious. Two women wearing black coats and gloves climbing over the fence into a dusty yard?"

"No time to worry about that now," Bee said, and clambered over. She landed, stumbled and caught herself.

"Ten points for elegance."

"Why thank you," she said.

I followed her, stumbled myself—I tripped and Bee caught me. "See? Not as easy as it looks," she said.

"I take back my initial assessment." I brushed myself off, resisting the urge to duck low. We were pretty much hidden from the road behind Misty's tall fence.

Bee walked to the front of the house and up the steps. She stopped, frowning at the bottles lying on their sides. "I don't mean to judge, but it looks like somebody might have had a problem."

"That doesn't mean anything, though," I said. "She could have had a drinking problem, but could that have anything to do with the murder?"

Bee tried the front door. "Locked. Do you have a hair pin?"

I fluffed my short brown hair. "Sorry, no. You're not seriously telling me you can pick the lock on the door?"

"Not now, anyway. Let's check the windows. You take that side of the house, and I'll try this one."

We split up and headed in opposite directions. I wasn't about to break a window to get into the house, but I tried every one. All of them were sash and locked tight, most with their curtains drawn.

"Here," Bee hissed from the corner of the house, gesturing frantically. "I found one."

I hurried after her, through the battered and dry flowerbeds and toward the other side of the house. Bee had found an open window into a bathroom.

"Boost me up," Bee said, "and I'll come around and open for you."

I formed a cradle with my hands, and Bee, who was meant to be in her 60s and not a gymnast, heaved herself through the window and slid out of sight, kicking her feet. Something broke inside the bathroom, and a few thumps sounded.

"Are you OK?" I whispered.

"Fine," she replied, in a strangled voice. "Go to the front door."

I scooted around to the front, nervous about breaking into and entering Misty's house.

The front door opened, and a waft of stale air drifted out. It smelled of dust and old milk.

"Wow," I said. "That smells..."

"Lovely, isn't it? Now, get in before someone sees you."

I entered and the floorboards in the house squeaked underfoot. There were two floors, and we split up again, Bee staying downstairs and me heading up and into Misty's bedroom. My nose tickled at the odd smells. The bed was made, the bright green spread neat, and a pair of

Misty's slippers waited at the foot of the bed. It kinda creeped me out—Misty had made her bed on the morning of her death and just never come back again.

"Get yourself together woman." I walked through the room. The boards didn't squeak here, except for one that rattled a little when stepped on—it was right next to Misty's bed. That had to have been annoying. Every time she got up, she would've heard it. I frowned and pressed my foot onto the board then stamped once. It sounded hollow.

"That's weird," I muttered, bending down and peeking under the bed. There was nothing under it, thankfully.

I placed my fingers on the loose board and pressed down on it again. It rattled. I knocked on it, and there was that hollow sound again. I inserted my fingers into the gap at the end of the board and gave a tug. It came free easily.

Would you look at that?

A decorative box had been secreted underneath the floorboards. I extracted it.

I got up and rushed to the door. "Bee," I called, allowing my voice to project, but not yelling. "You've got to see this."

Footsteps hurried through the house, and Bee appeared at the foot of the stairs. "What is it?"

"I found a box."

"A box?"

"Yes. Under the floorboards."

Bee was up the stairs like a bullet out of a gun.

We opened the box, standing over the gap next to the bed.

The secret trove was filled with stationery, envelopes, and a few letters. My heart tha-thumped in my chest. Stationery. And it looked similar to the style of letter I'd gotten.

"Hold this," I said, and handed her the box. I shoved my hand into my pocket and brought out the envelope.

Bee extracted one from the box, and we compared.

"The same," Bee said. "Curious."

"Downright weird. Do you think someone broke in and stole the stationery?"

"That or Misty's come back from the dead to taunt you," Bee said. "What are all of these anyway?" She extracted the notes that had been written on and paged through them. "Rubes, look at this." She gave me one.

I scanned the page and compared the handwriting to the letter I'd received from 'Daniel.' They weren't a match.

"Read it," Bee said, opening another.

Attention Miss. Kelly,

Your payments are overdue. If you want to continue this relationship, you'll have to pay up. That or the sensitive information you don't want revealed will come out.

M.

"Blackmail," I said. "Misty was blackmailing Harper."

"So, it wasn't just a punch up in the street. Harper said she'd only asked for money. She said nothing about blackmail."

"Exactly," I said.

Fifteen

I'D HOPED NEVER TO RETURN TO HARPER KELLY'S art gallery—a vain wish because my eyes couldn't take the brightness, and I just wasn't the type of person who hung around sipping champagne and chatting about expressive colors.

"Here we go again," Bee said, stopping in front of the gallery. The glass doors were open once again, but the gallery was quiet today. The counter near the front didn't hold its usual tray of champagne.

"Is it open?" I asked. "Silly question. Of course it is." I highly doubted Harper would've left the doors to the gallery ajar if she wasn't open for business.

"It's dark inside."

Bee was right. The interior of the gallery was dimmer than it had been the last time—and not just because of the paintings. The lights had been dimmed. I checked my watch. It was late afternoon, and the sun darted behind clouds and reappeared again in the slate-colored sky.

"Spooky," I said.

Bee rolled her eyes at me. "Come on, let's find her."

We entered and stopped just inside, a breeze tugging at our coats. Classical musical tinkled from the speakers as usual. We'd found Harper near the back last time, so I headed off in that direction. The colorful artwork was still there, but it wasn't as taxing on the eyes.

"Miss Kelly?" My voice rang through the empty space and bounced off the abstract shapes in their frames. "Miss Kelly, are you in here?"

"You'd think she'd have put up one of those 'back in five minutes' signs if she'd left."

"Very small town thing to do."

"Exactly." Bee wandered off to the left and disappeared behind some of the displays.

I headed toward a door at the back of the room. Possibly, it led into the office. Could Harper be in there? "Miss Kelly?" I rapped my knuckles on the polished wood. "Are you in there?" I tried the brass knob, but the office door was locked. "Shoot. Where is she?"

I circled back to the paintings with their shades of yellow and blue, wincing at their scrutiny. Apparently,

Harper liked eyes. Painting lots of them, at least. It was very 'Big Brother' and I held back a shiver.

The gallery was quiet. The tinkling piano music cut off.

What on earth?

"Bee?" I hissed. "Bee?" No answer.

Oh heavens, what now? My blood rushed in my ears, and I tiptoed forward, peering around the standing displays, just in case.

A clatter sounded from nearby, behind one of the displays, and my heart leaped into my throat.

I opened my mouth to call Bee's name again but no words would come out.

You can do this.

I fumbled in my purse for my pepper spray and brought it out with trembling fingers. I checked the nozzle was pointed in the right direction—away from me. Knowing my luck, I would wind up spraying myself and presenting an easy target for the killer.

It's not the killer. Relax.

The clatter came again then a muttering, shuffling noise around the back of a display.

This is it. On three.

Three, two, one...

I leaped around the side of the divider bringing up the pepper spray. "Freeze!"

Bee let out a yelp and hopped on the spot, lifting her hands. She lowered them again, glaring at me. "Ruby, what on earth are you doing? You scared my heart right out of my chest."

"What am I doing? What are you doing?" I tried not to stammer. "Why didn't you answer me? And what happened to the music?"

"I didn't hear you. And I tripped over the darn stereo cord thingy. It must've come out of the socket. I was kind of preoccupied, anyway." Bee gestured to the desk in front of her. She'd found her way to the reception area near the front and was behind it, messing around with the desk drawers.

"What are you doing?"

"Snooping. When the cat's away, the mice will play," Bee said. "And we're the mice. I have a feeling there might be a tasty bit of cheese in this drawer. We just have to be quick about it. But it's locked. You don't have a—?"

"No, Bee, I don't have a hairpin. We went over this already, remember?"

"Right." She fisted her hips. "Well, shoot."

"What about the computer?" I gestured to the laptop sitting on the desk right in front of her. If we were going to sleuth, and potentially get caught, we might as well do it right. "People keep everything on their computers. You never know what we might find."

"Can't figure out the password," Bee said, and kept fiddling with the desk. "By the way, were you really going to spray me?"

"If you were an evil murderer, definitely."

Bee grunted.

I squeezed past her and bent over the laptop, my gaze darting to the front of the gallery in case the assistant or Harper decided to reappear. I tapped my fingers on the keys.

If I was Harper's password, what would I be?

I tried the obvious combinations first, like '12345' and 'admin,' but no luck. Apparently Harper was more creative than that.

Think, Ruby. This is an art gallery computer. Or Harper's personal laptop that she carries around with her.

Creative. That was the keyword. But not the password. I wracked my brain, going over what Harper, Bee and I had talked about earlier in the week.

"Picasso," I whispered.

"Bless you," Bee replied.

"No, the password. I think I know what it might be." Harper had mentioned her inspiration for her lurid art had come from Picasso—who was turning in his grave somewhere. I typed the artist's name into the password box and hit enter. "Bingo. We're in."

"How did you do that?" Bee asked.

"Deductive reasoning."

"So, a lucky guess?"

"Pretty much." I opened up Harper's recent documents, but there was nothing of note, apart from a few accounts that were unpaid, judging by their 'final notice' print in bold at the top.

"Try her email," Bee said. "That's usually where all the juicy stuff is hidden." Bee shifted her weight from one foot to the other, switching out her gaze from the laptop to the street. "And hurry."

I opened up her email and scanned her inbox. Threatening emails took up most of it. I scrolled then switched through the other folders—spam, sent, and trash. An email waited in the 'trash' folder.

"Oh. Look at this."

Bee leaned in and we read the email together.

H.

Meet me at 10 in the church on Saturday. Use the side door. Delete after reading.

It wasn't signed by anyone, and the email address was a random combination of numbers from a yahoo account.

Bee and I exchanged a glance. "Tomorrow's Saturday."

A bang from the back of the gallery sent us scrambling to get out from behind the counter and into the street.

Saturday at 10. It seemed Harper Kelly had something

to hide, after all. I would've bet my last cupcake that it had to do with Misty's death.

97

Sixteen

The church was unlocked, the grand wooden doors thrown wide open every morning. We'd passed it in the food truck each time we'd gone to the lake to set up shop. Today was no different, of course, but it felt that way.

Butterflies—the non-romantic kind—made their intentions clear in my tummy as we approached the church. It was perfectly normal for two women to go to church on a Saturday at 10 am, but here I was. Worrying. Anxious.

"Ruby, you're pale."

"Sorry," I said, "I don't know what's gotten into me. I think it's just the combination of everything. The food truck being in for repairs and the mystery and now this... a clandestine meeting. What if it's got nothing to do with the murder?"

"Then we'll follow another lead," Bee said. "But, between you and me—"

"Who else would it be between?"

"—between you and me," Bee repeated, "I think we're about to get the clue we've been waiting for."

We circled around the rough stone side of the church and found the door the note had mentioned. "Here we go," I whispered.

Bee tried it then frowned. The heavy door didn't budge. "It's locked."

"Locked? But why would the person who sent the email have told Harper to come through the side door if it was locked?"

"Maybe it's a trap. They could be waiting in the…" Bee trailed off—there weren't bushes anywhere nearby, but there were trees much further back, across the green grass that the pastor clearly tended to. Or the gardener who worked for the church. Not that it mattered.

Heavens, my mind was all over the place.

"Let's go around the front," Bee said. "We can check out the side door from the inside. Besides, it's only 9:45 am. We're early."

Hopefully, Bee's explanation was correct. That or we'd

somehow gotten the wrong time? But no, the email had been clear. 10 am on Saturday.

We walked back around to the front of the church, arm-in-arm, and entered it. The inside of the church was gorgeous. A colored-glass window sat above the pulpit, and the pews were polished and decorated with the odd crimson cushion. The stone floor was accented by a central rug that trailed between the pews and led up to the front dais.

"Look at this place," I said. "It's so historical."

"It is." Bee said, looking up at the ceiling and the gallery of chairs above. "Big enough to seat the entire town."

I tugged on her arm, and we strode between the pews, our footsteps muted on the carpeting then loud on the stone. We headed for the side of the church, but the door there was still shut and the place was silent.

Bee and I waited in one of the pews, bowing our heads and darting glances to the supposed meeting spot, until fifteen minutes had passed. And then another five.

"Nothing," Bee said, checking her watch. "Did we get the time wrong? The meeting place?"

"No, we didn't. Maybe they called it off. Or maybe Harper decided she wasn't going to show."

"But then the one who organized the meeting would still be here."

"Right." I got up and walked to the side door of the church—it was sequestered in an alcove separate from the church's main worship area. I frowned, folding my arms and peering around at the empty section.

"What's that?" Bee asked, just as I'd spotted it.

A book had been left next to the door. A book I recognized. It had a thick, purple leather cover and the word 'journal' printed across its front.

"My diary," I said, and picked it up. I flipped it open, and a note fell from it.

Bee caught the letter before I could. "Hide this for me." Bee turned the note over. "That's all it says."

The dots connected, and I shook my head. The person who had broken into my truck was the same one who'd organized a meeting with Harper. And that person had probably written me the note as 'Daniel' as well. I flipped through my journal, and found a few entries had been marked with a folded corner of the page. They all had details of my history with Daniel, my fears and insecurities.

I flushed red-hot.

Who had done this? And why?

"We should go find Harper," Bee said. "She has to know what's going on. She's in on this."

"Shouldn't we speak to Detective Wilkes, first?"

"No. No, we shouldn't. Let's confront her. She'll know something, Ruby. We'll squeeze it out of her."

And that meant it was back to the gallery. At least, I wasn't anxious anymore. Now, I was downright angry. I'd come to the town to sell cookies and cupcakes and donuts, not to be targeted by murderers and whatever Harper was.

"It's OK," Bee said, patting me on the shoulder. "We'll find out who did this. Harper has to know."

I slapped my journal shut, slid it into my handbag, and followed her out of the church.

HARPER KELLY WAS NOWHERE TO BE FOUND. We'd tried the gallery, we'd checked the cafes and restaurants in town, and even asked Mrs. Rickleston at the front desk if she'd heard anything. The only option we had left was to contact our new glitzy friend, Lucy, but we didn't have her number and the nail salon closed early on a Saturday.

That was the only curse of small towns—it was never certain when places would be open, and there wasn't a convenience store to speak of here. Just a local 'market' that would order items in if they didn't have them. And that could take weeks.

"Let's take this out onto the back porch," Bee said, lifting her mug.

Mrs. Rickleston had set up a coffee and cakes station

next to the front desk. It was a popular addition, and I'd already grabbed myself two mini-lemon meringue tartlets and a cup of coffee. Bee held a jelly donut on her plate, and a cup of coffee too.

If we couldn't pin the murder on Harper or squeeze her for information, at least we could drown our sorrows in good coffee and treats.

The back porch of the inn was sheltered from the harsh wind, with an arrangement of outdoor armchairs and a lounging sofa facing the view of the grass and trees behind it. Birds chirped and flittered from branch-to-branch, and the sun, still hiding its shine behind clouds, was washed out when it did appear.

"Well," Bee said, taking a bite of her jelly donut. "That was a waste of time."

"I don't get it. Where could she be? People don't just disappear off the face of the earth. Unless she's gone into hiding because of that email she received?"

"She did delete it," Bee said.

"That's got to mean something."

"Hmm, it might mean that she was just following instructions. After all, that was what the guy said in the email—delete after opening or reading or whatever," Bee said. "Not that it's a guy. Maybe it was Olivia who sent it."

"Or O'Leary. He's the most suspicious out of everyone we've met so far. I mean, an ex-mob man? And he despised

Misty. Do we know who's inherited the bakery yet?" I asked.

"No news." Bee shook her head. "But it has to break sometime soon. The funeral's done and dusted."

"Poor choice of words."

Bee shrugged. "And from what Mrs. Rickleston has said, the family solicitor has been hovering around town."

"I hope that gives us another lead because this is ridiculous. We're hitting dead-ends no matter which way we go." I set down my coffee cup on the table between the armchairs and pinched the bridge of my nose. "What do you think about the meeting?"

"Which one? The fake Daniel one or the Harper one."

The fake meeting with whoever had written the note had passed. We didn't have enough information to confront whoever had written it yet, and the thought of going to meet a murderer scared me. I had a black belt in karate but faced with a gun or knife? That probably wouldn't mean much.

Better to let the meeting pass and focus on the case. If the murderer was persistent, assuming it was the murderer who'd written the note, they would try again.

Now, there was a sure-fire way to make a girl shiver.

"Harper," I prompted. "Why didn't she show up to the meeting? It can only mean that she ran away before it. I mean, she seems to have left her gallery in a rush?"

"Or she's just running errands."

"And no one's seen her this morning? That doesn't make sense."

Bee nodded. "What do we do now?"

"You're asking me? You're the ex-cop!"

"And you're the ex-investigative journalist. Boy, there's a mouthful." Bee finished off her donut and licked sugar off her lips. "We have to find Harper. That or we need to find out who she was meeting with."

"Yes, but there's no way to do that, is there?" An idea blinked to life like a lightbulb above my head. "Hold on a second." I grabbed my handbag from next to the chair and lifted it into my lap. I extracted the threatening note I'd received from 'Daniel.' "Do you still have the note that was in my journal at the church?"

"The 'hide this for me' note? Sure." Bee brought it out of her pocket and opened it up.

I took it from her and compared them. "Same handwriting," I said. "Look, see how the 'm' is shaped with the twirl on the end?"

"I see it," Bee said, "but all that tells us is that the person who wrote the fake note is the same one who stole your journal."

"And broke into the truck. And they're friends with Harper. And—"

A plangent *meow* sounded from the end of the porch. I blinked. Good heavens, that was loud.

I opened my mouth to continue my thought, but the meow came a second time.

"Does Mrs. Rickleston have any cats?" I asked.

"Not that I can remember."

I got up and searched for the kitty. It sat next to the porch, white as snow, its yellow eyes blinking up at me. It meowed again then hunched into position for a jump and wiggled its furry butt. It leaped up onto the porch railing and pranced back and forth meowing impetuously.

"Hello," I said. "How are you?" I put out a hand.

The kitty-cat sniffed it, turned up its nose and continued its pacing on the porch-rail.

"Friendly, isn't it?" Bee laughed. "Nothing like our Trouble."

Trouble had been the kitten at the last guesthouse we'd stayed in. But this snowy-white cat didn't have collar or tag. And it wasn't interested in being touched by me. Each time I reached out, it batted at my hand or hissed.

"I think it's a stray," I said. "Maybe we should take it to the vet?"

"That's if you can get your hands on it without it scratching them off."

"You wouldn't hurt me, would you, kit?" I put out my hand, and the cat's paw slashed out. Its claws scratched burning lines into my skin. I snatched my arm to my side. "All right, so you may have a point. But it wants something."

"Food, most likely." Bee rose. "I'll get some shredded chicken from Mrs. Rickleston, and ask her if she's seen this cat before."

I waited with the increasingly loud and potentially anxious kitty until Bee came back with two bowls. One with water and one with shredded chicken. She set them down on the porch then we both backed up and sat down to watch the cat.

It stared at us, flicking its tail, then leaped down and started eating.

"There," Bee said. "Just hungry. Mrs. Rickleston said that it's the cat of a deceased guest."

"What? That's horrible."

"Yeah, apparently the cat had gone missing a day or two before the woman died. And they couldn't find it again. It turns up once in a while for food but never stays long enough for Mrs. Rickleston to contact the woman's family. They live in Chicago."

"Oh no."

The kitty ate noisily, finally purring.

"Does she know its name?"

"Snowy," Bee said. "It's a girl cat."

"Snowy." I lifted my voice. "Snowy, here kitty."

Snowy paused her chicken evisceration to stare at me. She blinked, sneezed, then returned to her meal.

"Well, I think she should see a vet, just to be sure she's not sick or anything," I said. "We'll have to soften her up somehow to get her into a cat carrier."

"We'll have to get a cat carrier."

It was the least of our worries at the moment, what with the food truck out of commission and the murderer on the loose, but with no leads, helping Snowy would be a worthy distraction. Besides, she was spunky. I liked that.

Snowy finished her meal, took a few sips of water then leaped back onto the railing and over the other side. She trotted off across the lawn and disappeared between some trees.

"Maybe next time," I said.

I had the suspicious feeling that I might be saying that about this murder investigation. If we didn't find Harper Kelly soon.

Seventeen

THAT NIGHT, I LAY IN BED WITH A BOOK OPEN ON my lap, twiddling my toes under the covers and frowning. I'd reread the same line about ten times, and that wasn't like me. I was the type who disappeared into books without much prompting. My room was as small and sweet as ever, comfortable and warm, with a fire that had been lit in the fireplace by the turndown service, but I couldn't get cozy.

It's the meeting. It doesn't make any sense.

I sighed and pinned my finger between the book's pages, casting a glance over at the alarm clock on my bedside table.

9 pm.

I narrowed my eyes at the pearly white face of the alarm clock. 9 pm. Why did that seem important?

Relax, you're too stressed.

But no, there was something important about that time. Wasn't there? I found my book marker, slipped it between the pages, and set my book aside, nudging the clock.

"You need to sleep. It's getting late." The lecture did nothing to relax me. I swung my feet over the edge of the bed and put on my slippers. "Late. Not early." The words left my mouth, and I frowned, tilting my head to one side. "Late. Not early."

What had the email said?

That Harper was to meet the mystery sender at the church at ten. And to use the side door. But we'd been there at 10 am and nothing had happened. Harper hadn't shown up. The book had been waiting, but Harper and the person, whoever, they were, hadn't been anywhere to be found.

I sucked in a gasp.

Of course!

"Not morning. Night!" I leaped out of bed and ran out into the hall. I hammered my fists on Bee's door. "Bee! Wake up! Bee?"

Bee's door opened, and she stood holding it, her hair in disarray, a sleeping mask shoved up onto her forehead. "Are you trying to wake the dead?"

"No, but Bee—"

"So just the entire inn then."

"It wasn't in the morning."

"Huh?"

"The meeting! The meeting wasn't meant to be at 10 am, it was supposed to be at 10 pm. We just assumed it was in the morning because... well, I don't know why. Because we just went with it."

Bee's scowl evaporated. "What time is it?"

"It's just past nine."

"I'll meet you downstairs in five minutes," Bee said, and slapped the door shut in my face.

I didn't have a problem with the rudeness. I was too excited about what was to come—catching Harper and her accomplice in action.

BEE AND I WORE OUR ALL-BLACK OUTFITS WITH matching gloves, even though it felt a little ridiculous sneaking through the park, past the duck pond and along the lamp lit pathways toward the opposite street. The church loomed through the semi-darkness.

"Are you ready for this?" I asked.

"Born ready," Bee replied.

The church drew closer and closer, and with it, my anxiety heightened. Who were we about to see meeting with Harper? Was Harper even there at all? Or had she already been 'disposed of' by the murderer.

Not that it was necessarily the murderer who had written the note. But who else would it have been?

Get control of your crazy thoughts, woman.

We reached the front of the church and slipped through the open gates. They were never locked, but this time, the front doors of the church were shut tight.

Bee and I moved into single file and moved around the side of the church, toward the door that had been closed earlier. It was ever-so-slightly open now. Light spilled from within, but it had a flickering quality. Candlelight? A fire?

I signaled to Bee, and she gestured for me to go on ahead.

The soft rumble of someone talking came from within the church, but it didn't seem near to the door, so I took my chance and slipped inside. The separate little alcove was empty—the flickering light came from between the pews nearby, or from one in particular.

Bee came in behind me, and we positioned ourselves, skirting toward the pillars that separated the pew area from the side alcove. I peered out from behind one and forced myself not to gasp.

Pastor Jack Byrne sat next to Harper on one of the

pews. A flickering candle had been placed on the end of the pew, casting light over their meeting.

"—don't understand what you mean," Harper said.

I checked my watch. It was just past 10 pm now. Thankfully, our trek across the park had delayed us. Who knew what would've happened if we'd arrived at the same time as Harper.

"Darling, you must understand. I left it right by the door for you," Jack said.

Darling?

Puzzle pieces clicked into place—Jack was having an affair with Harper! He was the pastor and had a loyal wife. If Misty would've blackmailed Harper about anything, it had to be that.

Hold your horses. Maybe he's just being endearing to a member of his 'flock.'

Jack lifted Harper's hand from her lap and kissed the back of it, gently. "I don't want to get angry with you, dear."

"Angry with me? Listen, I arrived and there was nothing by the door. If there was, I'd have it with me right now. Besides, why didn't you just give whatever it was to me here? We're already sitting with each other."

"I don't want to risk it," Jack said. "I had to wipe it down."

"Wipe what down?" Harper asked, exasperation in her tone.

"The book. The journal. That snooping baker's journal. Remember? The one I told you I'd gotten my hands on?"

"You mean stole," Harper said. "I still don't think you should have done that."

"I just wanted to make sure she wasn't planning anything bad. We don't want another Misty situation on our hands." Jack kissed her other fingers, and I held back a tide of nausea.

How could he do this to his wife? And to the people who came to church? People trusted this man. If he was having an affair, and he'd clearly broken into my truck and stolen my journal and case notes, what else was he capable of?

"Why do you want me to have the journal?" Harper asked. "I don't want anything to do with this. I had enough trouble with Misty. Can you believe the police actually questioned me about it?"

"You didn't tell them anything about us, did you?"

"Of course not, Jack. I'm not stupid," Harper replied. "But I am getting tired of hiding everything. I wish you would just leave her once and for all. Then we could be together. We could be happy."

Jack brushed his fingers over her cheek. "You know I

can't do that. Besides, we wouldn't have the money to run away together."

"But I can help with that, I told you."

Jack shook his head. "I don't have any money of my own. If my bank account had a bigger balance then maybe..."

"Is that all that's keeping you from leaving with me?" Harper asked. "We could move to New York together. To SoHo! I'll transfer money into your account if that's how you feel."

"Maybe," he said, and drew her into a hug.

"I think I'm going to throw up," Bee breathed.

I go the odd feeling that Harper would do better to *not* give Jack any money. The whole situation was strange. He had broken into my truck and viciously gutted my upholstery, just because he wanted the diary? It had seemed more like a warning.

"The journal is probably by the door, dear," Jack said. "You just missed it. Why don't you go check if it's there? I'll wait."

Ice flooded my veins.

Harper incoming.

"Do I have to?"

"Yes, dear. It's important."

"Fine." The pew creaked.

I twirled my finger at Bee and pointed to the side door.

We rushed out, half-running, half-tiptoeing, holding our breaths. We darted across the church yard.

I looked back every few steps, but Harper didn't follow us out, and the sliver of light leaking from the door remained the same until I ran around the corner and into the night.

$$\mathcal{E}ighteen$$

"Harper doesn't seem to know anything other than the fact that Jack needs money," I said, pacing back and forth in the entry-hall of the inn. We'd only just gotten back, but the place was quiet, and the coffee station was empty. We'd have no luck getting any now, not here, unless I headed into the kitchen and snooped around.

"Let's talk about this somewhere else," Bee said.

"Upstairs?"

"No, outside, on the back porch," she said. "I'll run upstairs and get my phone. Make us each a hot cocoa and bring it down. Sound good?"

"Yes." It would give me time to brainstorm. Thankfully, there were hot cocoa stations in our rooms for our convenience.

Bee hurried off, and I took a calmer stroll through the

inn and to the back porch. I opened the door and let myself out, finding a seat on the same armchair as earlier. The porch lights were on, but they hardly shed light further than the back steps.

Harper was being blackmailed about her relationship. Jack felt threatened by it. Could he have taken the next step?

Bee reappeared with her phone and two mugs of cocoa about five minutes later. She handed me a cup, and I took it, gratefully, blowing on the top then drawing some sweetness into my mouth. How surreal, we'd been sneaking through a church just a few minutes ago, and now we were here, sipping cocoa and talking about the results of our investigation.

"Why did you need your phone?" I'd been so caught up in the whole Harper-Jack affair, I hadn't bothered asking.

"I'm calling a buddy of mine in Boston. He might be able to help me with the case."

"How?" I asked.

"Let's just say, he's a cop who knows things he shouldn't. And if there's anything we need to know about this Jack guy, he'll know about it."

"Are you sure?" I asked. "I don't see how he'd know anything if Jack is part of Muffin and he's not a cop here."

"Trust me," Bee said. "My friends are not only in high places, they're highly intelligent." She got up and paced to the other end of the porch, where we'd run into the kitty cat, Snowy, earlier. Her bowls were still there, empty now. She tapped on her phone screen then placed it to her ear.

"Well, here we go," I murmured.

Would Bee find out anything new about Jack? Maybe not, but it was worth a shot, and my suspicions had grown about both Harper and the pastor. It just didn't sit right with me, a pastor having an affair like that.

He could've been capable of—

"Dirk," Bee said. "Sorry to call so late." Her tone was businesslike. "Yeah, yeah, it's been a while. Listen, I need some help here. I've got a person if interest and I need to know what you know. Know what I meant?"

"That's a lot of knowing things," I whispered to myself.

"Right. Pastor Jack Byrne." Bee turned away from the railing and met my gaze. "Yeah, you heard me right. He's not? Not at all? Really. Now, that's interesting. Well, thanks for your time, Dirk. Talk soon." She hung up.

"That's it?" I asked.

Bee pocketed her phone and sat down. "That's interesting."

"What did he say?"

"Jack isn't a pastor. He's got a rap sheet as long as forever. He's a complete conman and, apparently, he's wanted in Boston for a previous murder. Dirk is getting in contact with his superiors and the detective here, right now."

"So, he'll be brought down either way. But what if he wasn't the one who—"

Heavy footsteps thumped around the side of the inn, and a dark figure sprinted into view.

I gripped Bee's arm. She got up, and I went with her.

The figure came into the light.

Pastor Jack Byrne, or rather, the conman, Jack Byrne strode up the back steps of the quaint clapboard inn and stopped in front of us. He wore his black shirt, minus the white clerical collar. He tilted his head to one side, tucking his hands into the pockets of his pants. "Hello, ladies."

"Pastor," I said, nodding.

"Harper tells me you were sneaking around the church tonight," he said. "Any particular reason for that?"

"No idea what you're talking about," Bee said. "We've been here."

"That must be why you're both wearing all black." He drew a gun out of his pocket and pointed it at me. "The game's over. You know I killed Misty. You've figured it out."

"Actually, no, we hadn't quite reached that conclusion yet," Bee said.

"We had our suspicions though," I put in. "Thanks for confirming them." I'd gone cold all over, and it had nothing to do with the rolling clouds above nor the first spatters of rain on the grass in the back yard. He was *here*. "Misty knew you weren't a pastor. It wasn't just about the affair, was it?"

"Misty liked to stick her nose where it didn't belong. She was a sneak. Always trying to find the worst in people. Always looking for dirt to use."

"And she found it," Bee said.

"Correct. By going through my things. But that doesn't matter now." He shifted the gun toward Bee then back to me again. "You won't know anything by the end of tonight, and Harper? Well, shoot, she's my meal ticket out of here. She'll give me what I need, and I'll be on my way. Mexico here I come." He hooted the last part.

My gaze fixed on the gun, glinting by the light from the wall sconce.

What could we do?

If I screamed for help, he'd shoot one of us. If I tried to reason with him, he—

A scratching noise sounded, and Snowy the cat leaped up onto the railing next to the fake pastor. He didn't seem to notice.

"Any last words?"

"That's so cliché," Bee said.

"Suit yourself." Jack swung the weapon toward her.

Snowy let out another of her incredibly loud meows

and leaped onto the fake pastor's hand. She dug her kitty claws into his flesh and brought her fangs down on his knuckles.

Bee and I dived aside.

Jack screamed and stumbled backward, dropping his gun. Snowy leaped onto Jack's head and went into full kitty attack mode.

"The gun!" Bee yelled.

I skidded across the rough floorboards and grabbed the gun. I brought it up and directed it at the murderer. He ran around in circles in the back yard, screaming as Snowy ravaged his head, and rain fell from the laden clouds above.

Finally, Snowy released him and rushed off into the trees, but it was too late. Jack's face was streaked with blood from the attack, and he wore a look halfway between fury and terror.

That cat just saved our lives.

I pointed the gun at Jack, Bee stepping up to join me on the right. "Don't move," I said, "the cops are on their way."

Another murderer caught, another case solved. Would we ever find peace?

At this point, I'm not sure I want to.

Nineteen

The following Monday

"Here Snowy," I cooed, holding out the bowl of shredded chicken. "Here girl. Come on kitty cat, it's OK. It's just me."

Snowy sat, aloof and suspicious, atop the porch railing, eying my offering as if it would come to life and scratch her on the nose. Heavens, not that she couldn't defend herself. This cat was the sawed off shotgun of cats. She had taken down a murdering conman singlehandedly. Or was it... singlepawedly?

"Come on, sweetheart." I held the bowl.

Over the past two days, I'd been practicing getting her to come closer each time I brought out the food. I liked this girl's gumption. If I'd been able to take a cat with me on the food truck, I would've, but cats were terrible when it came to adapting to new environments.

That didn't mean we couldn't make friends. Mrs. Rickleston had already mentioned she'd like to have Snowy as the Runaway Inn's cat. After all, wasn't snowy technically a runaway? Much like Bee and me.

"Fine," I said, and put the bowl down. "But I'm not leaving this time." I sat down a short distance away from the chicken.

Snowy flicked her tail but hopped down from the railing and came to eat the chicken. She chewed neatly, letting out appreciative purrs and giving me the side-eye. I didn't dare touch her yet. Just the fact that she'd let me sit next to her while she ate was a sign of trust. I wasn't about to ruin that by moving too quickly.

The back door to the inn opened. "There you are," Bee said. "I've got good news."

"Anything to do with the murder?"

"Nope. That's done, Ruby. Jack's behind bars, Harper's already closed her gallery and is speaking with the cops about being an accomplice to the crime. Olivia has inherited her sister's bakery, and Tom O'Leary? Well, no one knows much about the guy."

"Thanks for the suspect rundown," I said, keeping my tone even so I wouldn't freak out Snowy. She'd already flicked her tail at Bee's sudden appearance. "But if it's not good news about the murder then what can it be?"

"The food truck's here!" Bee cried. "We can restock and get back to the lake by tomorrow. I'm thinking we'll do... hmm, what about choc chip cookies?"

"That's amazing." I didn't move a muscle.

"You're not exactly jumping for joy."

"Snowy's eating."

"Oh," Bee said. "I see. Well, any time you're—"

A massive bang sounded from the front of the inn. Snowy gave me a reproachful look, a loud meow, and leaped onto the railing and out of sight.

"Oh great," I sighed. "There goes all my hard work. What *was* that?"

"Someone arriving?"

I followed Bee inside the inn, happier than I'd been in days. Not only was I making some progress with Snowy, but we'd gotten our truck back, now, and the local residents were at their friendliest. Shoot, even Olivia had come by the inn to thank us for capturing her sister's killer. And she hadn't even liked Misty.

The inn's front doors were open, but a collection of bags had been dumped in them, blocking entry or exit. Mrs. Rickleston hovered nearby, appearing distressed.

"What's going on?" I asked.

"Oh, hello, Ruby," the innkeeper said. "Goodness, my

new guests had arrived I knew they would be a large party, but I didn't expect this."

A group of nearly identical looking blonde girls and brunette boys—sort of like a Brady bunch collection—strode up the inn's front steps. They chatted with each other and dumped another set of bags. They were young adults and teens, with two adults who had to be the parents among them.

"Wow," I said.

"There's got to be about twenty of them." Bee's eyes were wide.

"Twenty-two," Mrs. Rickleston replied. "The Flatley clan."

"Like Michael Flatley? Lord of the Dance?"

"Not related, but the name, yes, I suppose, dear," Mrs. Rickleston.

"Hey, move, you idiot." One of the teen boys pushed a girl fight, and a screeching slap fight ensued.

"Don't worry, dears. I'll make sure your stay at the inn is just as peaceful as ever."

That wasn't much of a promise, after what we'd been through the past little while. Bee and I exchanged a glance. "Looks like it's going to be another interesting few weeks," Bee said.

When wasn't it interesting when it came to us?

"Come on," I said, "let's go around the side of the inn. I'm itching to get baking again."

"You? Well, miracles do happen." Bee winked at me.

We looped arms and set off back down the hall, our backs to the commotion and turmoil and our gazes set on the future, and whatever else Muffin had planned for us.

Hopefully, not another murder.

Ruby and Bee's adventures continue in CHOC CHIP MURDER. Join them as they uncover yet another mystery.

If it's not in your local book store or library, be sure to request it from them!

Turn the page to read the first chapter!

More for you...

Sign up to my mailing list and receive updates on future releases, as well as **FREE** copies of *The Hawaiian Burger Murder* and *The Fully Loaded Burger Murder*.

They are *s*hort cozy mystery featuring characters from *the Burger Bar Mystery series.*

Head over to www.rosiepointbooks.com to sign up!

Craving More Cozy Mystery?

If you had fun with Ruby and Bee, you'll want to meet Sunny and her Aunt Rita's cat, Bodger. You can read the first chapter of Sunny's story below!

The cat was out to get me.

It sat on the top step of my auntie's cottage, its black paws placed neatly beside each other, its yellow eyes focused on me. Every time I tried taking a step up the front path, it would hiss, fur standing on end.

Now, I hadn't exactly been expecting a welcome wagon when I'd arrived in Parfait, Florida, at the crack of dawn, but this was ridiculous. An angry cat, humidity that had no right to exist at 5:00 a.m., and the depressing realization that all my belongings fit into one wheeled suitcase —boy, was I living the life.

I cleared my throat, and the cat flicked its tail.

Why had Aunt Rita never told me she owned a cat? Though, in this case, it seemed more like the cat was the one who did the owning.

"Auntie," I warbled. "I'm here!"

She'd expected me two days ago, but paying my ex-husband's debts had taken longer than I'd hoped. There had been complications. People who I hadn't even known had had dealings with Damon had come out of the wood-work, looking for handouts. A lot of them were Russian. And intimidating. And had told me if I called the cops, I would regret it.

Try not to get depressed this early in the morning.

"Auntie Rita?" I called.

The cat hissed at me again.

"Oh relax," I said to it, hoping that my shouting hadn't woken the neighbors. Parfait was a small, coastal town, and the last thing I wanted was to make enemies on arrival. According to Aunt Rita, the locals adored her café and were pretty laid back, unless you got on their bad side.

I took a breath and fiddled with the extended handle of my suitcase. This was absurd. I couldn't let a cat get in my way. Aunt Rita had invited me to stay at her house while I got back on my feet after the messiest, scariest divorce in history.

And, yeah, I had been through the wringer, but I

wasn't about to let a feline with an attitude problem prevent me from having a good start to my "revival."

Granted, my revival had so far comprised three sweaty bus rides and being hit on by a toothless man who smelled of bourbon and peanut butter. Interesting combination, I'd give him that.

"Aunt Rita." I tried one last time.

The cat meowed, showing off disastrously sharp fangs.

"Look," I said, directing myself to the cat, "I like cats. Pretty much every animal is great in my books, barring chickens. Long story." I waved a hand. "The bottom line is, I'm expected, OK? Aunt Rita knows I'm coming, so you can chill out."

Another disdainful flick of the tail.

Grow a pair of ovaries, Sunny, for heaven's sake. What's the worst that could happen? It launches at your ankles?

I *did* have tender ankles.

"OK," I said, "I'm coming up."

The cat had understood that, it seemed, because it rose on all fours and yowled like a bat out of the nether. It hissed and spat, clawing as I walked up the cute path that led to Aunt Rita's single-story cottage.

"Shoo!" I waved a hand. "Shoo!"

The cat streaked toward me, and I braced for clawed impact. It disappeared underneath a bush rather than inflicting flesh wounds.

"Huh, would you look at that," I murmured. "All hiss and no claws." I trudged up the front steps, grinning at my silly idiom, and stopped on the cutesy, floral-print welcome mat.

I rapped my knuckles on the front door. "Aunt Rita?" It was early, but my aunt usually rose with the birds. She had when I'd lived with her, and I doubted that habit had changed over the last twenty years. Shoot, every Christmas I visited she'd wake me up with coffee at 4:30 a.m..

Twenty years. Gosh, was I really *that* old?

Thirty-eight and back at Auntie's house, looking for a place to stay, broke as the day I left.

I knocked. "It's me, Sunny." Still no answer.

The house was quiet as the grave.

Uh oh. OK, no need to panic.

My aunt always kept a spare key in plain sight in case she wasn't home when I came to visit. She'd changed her hiding spot from under the mat to the potted plant hanging from the eaves about a year ago. That was after I'd pointed out that everyone kept their spare key under the welcome mat.

I dug around in the soil in the potted plant and extracted the key. I dusted it off, my nerves building.

Why wasn't she answering the door? And why was her cat acting so weird? And when on earth had she gotten a cat?

I let myself into the cottage's entrance hall. It smelled faintly of lavender and chocolate chip cookies, as it always did. The evil cat streaked past me into the house, hissing for good measure, and I shut the door.

"Auntie?" I called out and flicked on the lights.

The place was immaculate—polished wood floors, styled in teal and cream, with framed pictures of me and Aunt Rita along the walls, showing my progression from geeky teenager to woman.

"Where is she?" I scooted my bag into place next to an end table. My gaze landed on an envelope propped against a vase of flowers. My name was scrawled across the front in my aunt's looping handwriting.

I lifted it, frowning. Why would she leave me a letter and not call me if she had a reason for not being here? Then again, I was a few days late.

I slit the envelope open with my aunt's silver letter opener and slipped out a single sheet of folded parchment paper.

My heart tha-thumped in my chest.

Dear Darling Sunny,

If you're reading this letter, I'm long gone. I regret to inform you that I've decided to go on a cruise with a few lady friends. To the Bahamas! Can you imagine it? Me in the Bahamas, sipping Bahamian drinks and dipping my toes in the water.

Now, you might think I'm crazy for leaving Florida, which is basically a prime vacation destination, but I need a break.

It's for this reason that I'm leaving you in charge of the Sunny Side Up Café until I get back.

I nearly dropped the letter in shock. "What?" I had no experience running a business whatsoever. I had gone to college to get a business degree, but my studies had been cut short when I'd married Damon. Besides, I couldn't cook a meal to save my life! Except for maybe spaghetti, and even that was touch and go.

I straightened the page and kept reading.

Don't worry, dear, you'll have plenty of help. Just try not to burn the place down while I'm gone.

I'll be unreachable for a few days until we've settled in, at which point you'll be able to contact me via the number on the back of this letter.

Have fun! Live a little!

Sincerely,

Aunt Rita

P.S. I've already had my neighbors feeding Bodger, but if you could take over from them once you arrive, that would be perfect. Also, Bodger hates everyone except for me, so make sure to lock your bedroom door at night. He has a tendency to leap at people's faces when they close their eyes.

Each word in the letter was worse than the last.

I was alone in my aunt's house with a homicidal cat and a café to run. Talk about out of my depth. And what had she meant about having plenty of help?

A knock rattled the front door, and I jumped and nearly dropped the letter.

Want to read more? You can grab **the first book, MURDER OVER EASY,** on every major retailer!